You Can't Always Get What You Want

You Can't Always Get What You Want

A Young Adult Novel

Enjoy!

Carol Thorsness

CAROL THORSNESS

authorHOUSE®

AuthorHouse™
1663 Liberty Drive
Bloomington, IN 47403
www.authorhouse.com
Phone: 1-800-839-8640

Published by AuthorHouse 11/25/2014

ISBN: 978-1-4969-5462-6 (sc)
ISBN: 978-1-4969-5461-9 (e)

Library of Congress Control Number: 2014920880

Dedicated to
Chuck, Adam, Jeremy, Tina, Holly
Evelyn and Isabel
loves and inspirations

I was sitting at an author's luncheon listening to a local author describe the editing process and thinking, "That's fine, but first you need a plot..a beginning, a middle and an end." I had many beginnings filed away in drawers and a couple middles. I even had a beginning and an end called "*My Mother's Room*" but the middle just wouldn't come.

That's when Jake, Jamal, and Jamal's grandmother's walked into my head: beginning, middle and end. With them came almost an urgency to put them down on paper. Yes, I needed paper, two spiral notebooks, not the computer, to write their story. MaryEllen was there as was Ms Truwell, but they were hanging back until the pencil hit the pad.

Devon showed up as I was running one morning and demanded to be a part of it all. The Davis family all demanded to be a real part of the story not just background characters as originally intended.

As strange as it sounds, I wrote *You Can't Always Get What You Want* because I wanted to read it, and I hope you enjoy meeting these characters as much as I did.

CHAPTER ONE

Jake ambled into the Double R Tavern at five as was his custom. He ordered a cheeseburger, fries and a Sierra Nevada on draft because it was Thursday. Nodded a hello to Duke behind the bar and made his way to the booth close to the kitchen door in the back. The Double R was a prototype west Texas small town bar. When Duke bought it back in the sixties, he decided it looked just fine and reordered rather than redecorated. Well, that wasn't totally true. He considered the neon Pyramid Beer sign given to him by the sales rep in 1999 to have brought his place into the new millenium.

Jake was looking at the Pyramid sign now though not really seeing it. He was trying to decide whether or not he had enough time after dinner to stop by Les Anderson's office to pay the vet what he owed for his last ranch call. Les had helped usher in one of his new calves that didn't seem to want to come into the world. After 15 hours of hard labor, Jake wondered that the mama had even wanted to see her offspring let along suckle. But within minutes of dropping, all seemed forgiven and forgotten, and mama nestled her baby. The wonder of it seemed lost to Les. Maybe he had seen it too often.

Jake's glance was pulled from the sign down to the white haired woman coming toward him. She carried a draft in one hand and an iced tea in the other. Oh, oh, he was in trouble. Jake could not remember when MaryEllen had last bought him or anyone a beer, probably because she never had. Boy, oh boy, what did she want because with that crocked smile and the sloshing brew, she sure wanted something from him, something big.

"Well, hi there, Jake. It's so good to see you."

"Hello, Mayor Jenkins. What can I do for you?"

"Why, Jake, I just thought I'd buy you a Sierra Nevada. That's what you drink, right? And we'd have ourselves a little conversation."

Lord have mercy....a conversation? What could this be about? Too bad he'd brought his checkbook with him so that he could pay Les. He didn't have that excuse, but then, truth be told, Jake was always generous when it came to the town's needs. He'd given a sizable sum to update the library last fall and then wrote another check for the same amount to insure that library hours wouldn't be cut. These gifts were anonymous. But, of course, MaryEllen knew everything about her town, anonymous or not.

He looked at MaryEllen's beaming, wrinkled face. She must have been quite a beauty in her prime which to Jake's quick calculation was around the middle of the sixteenth century. She had been mayor of Clayton Springs for over twenty years. No one wanted – nor dared – to run against her in all that time. She was nosy, indefatigable, bossy, competent and unfailingly kind. Citizens of Clayton

Spring were very often annoyed with her but always loved her.

Twenty two years ago, MaryEllen's son, daughter-in-law and twin granddaughters died in a fiery crash at the corner of Downey and Main....the Jenkin's car versus a gas truck at 10 AM one beautiful Saturday spring morning. No blame was assigned by the investigating officers, but a recommendation that a 4 way stop be put in at that intersection was submitted and filed. After grieving her enormous loss and waiting, and waiting for action on the recommendation, MaryEllen found new purpose. She started with a petition for the 4 way stop to be put in and gathered over three thousand signatures. It went nowhere. so she ran for and became mayor with her first official duty to sign the funding for stoplights at Downey and Main.

Once that was accomplished, MaryEllen gathered up the entire town of Clayton Springs to be her family to care for and nurture, and that she had been doing for the last five elections cycles. Her small ranch south of town took little of her time. She lost most of her interest in it when Don and the girls died. She moved out of the main house, selling off most of her furniture and memories in a big estate sale, into the foreman quarters and gave the main house and the ranching responsibilities to her foreman Conner and his wife Sarah. It worked out well for all concerned especially since Sarah loved to cook and supplied MaryEllen with most of the meals she didn't eat at Checkerboard Cafe or McDonald's....she loved getting a senior coffee and a double cheeseburger on Wednesdays for just $2.49. She ignored the "senior" aspect to the coffee and just enjoyed getting a bargain meal.

Jake tried to figure how much MaryEllen's "conversation" was going to cost him. The check from the oil company's lease on the east 12 acres of his property had just come in so he was pretty flush. How did she know? He sighed. MaryEllen knew everything. Just as he was mentally bracing himself to write the biggest check he had ever written, MaryEllen switched from her lopsided grin to her motherly/grandmotherly-- "I'll help you do the right thing, trust me face."

"Now Jake, don't worry. I'm not gonna ask you for money"

Mental note – never play poker with MaryEllen.

Jake relaxed for a nano second and then really began to panic. Oh no, I do not want to be on the school board. I know Herman is retiring, but what do I know about Clayton Springs' schools? The Farm Bureau? I do my part there. Why doesn't she just want some money?

"Jake, I have a proposition I want you to consider. Clayton Springs is in a partnership program with Dallas. We have agreed to take an at-risk teenager for the summer to get him or her away from gangs and expose them to a different environment."

She looked intently into Jake's eyes.

"Now hold on, I want you to just listen and consider.. The young man who will be coming to our town lives with his grandmother in a Dallas barrio. He doesn't belong to a gang though I hear the pressure is as high to join as is the risk of not joining. He was highly recommend by his teachers and the principal of his school. You would have him for a little over two months starting Tuesday week. Jamal is thirteen and going into eighth grade next year. He wants to come. Think about it."

The last seven sentences seemed to be delivered in one breath and before Jake could tell MaryEllen how ridiculous it was to think he could take care of a kid for the summer, she was out the door.

Jake stared at the glass of half drunk ice tea. The beads on condensation on the glass matching the beads of sweat on his top lip. He took a deep breath, drained his first beer and then the one MaryEllen had brought. The rest of his cheeseburger had lost its appeal. As much as he wanted to dismiss MaryEllen's proposal out of hand for being just plain insane, which it was, he would do as she asked.... consider.

"Measure twice, cut once" was his dad's slogan. Though it was meant for carpentry, it applied to just about everything.

CHAPTER TWO

The next morning as Jake was scrambling his eggs, he looked around the ranch house kitchen. It was neat and clean, the way his mom had kept it, and the way Jake had kept it these eight years since her passing. There were three chairs around the kitchen table. He forked his eggs onto the plate beside the whole wheat toast, poured a cup of coffee, added a little sweet cream, and sat down in the chair with the view of the backyard, henhouse and south pasture. The Chronicle covered half the table, but he had to admit, there was room enough, and eggs enough, for a 13 year old.

After breakfast Jake wiped down the table, put his dishes into the dishwasher and grabbed two deviled ham sandwiches he had made yesterday. He tucked them, a couple apples and a water bottle into his saddlebags. He needed to check the well casing at the far side of the south pasture. It had started to crack and he needed to be sure it would function to water his herd during the upcoming hot summer months.

As he saddled Ben he looked over at Sadie, his Mom's horse. She was a good, gentle old mare and he needed to take her out for some exercise. Maybe she would do for an inexperienced 13 year old.

And so it went through the week with Jake noting situations that might fit with a teenager. Dang. He liked his uncomplicated life, but, then, it was only two months and there was enough on his west Texas ranch to keep a 13 year old---to keep Jamal busy for the summer.

Monday Jake drove over to Mike's house for their biweekly poker game. Mike had chips and salsa out with beer in the frig. They played in Mike's "man cave" as Ginger, Mike's wife called it. It was a comfortable air conditioned room Mike had built behind his garage workshop for playing poker and watching football games. Ginger had gone to a chick flick at the Cinemax with her three Weight Watcher girlfriends. They started their dinner-and-a-movie-every-other-Monday about 5 years ago. They joined Monday night Weight Watchers. After the weigh-in and meeting, they went out for salads at a cafe and then the movie. They stopped going to the WW meetings about four and a half years ago, but kept up with the dinner and a movie girls' night out.

"Ginger left us some brownies," Mike said as he lifted a very gooey two inch frosted square. Mike ate anything and everything and at six feet only weighed about 170 much to Ginger's dismay. Mike liked Ginger just as she was, never noticing when she went up 10 pounds or down 5. He sympathized with his wife's "metabolism troubles" whenever she brought it up. Otherwise he was just please when he came home to chocolate chips cookies, pecan pie or her wonderful frosted binge brownies.

"Nate's not coming. Sissy and the girls have a bug and he's the vomit squad."

Nate was Jake's best friend since elementary school. He hadn't seen much of him lately. When he married Sissy and had the girls, he became a real family man. Sissy liked Jake and had tried to set him up with a number of her girlfriends, but the set-ups just didn't work out and after a while Sissy had no more women friends who were still single.

John and Chris came in and grabbed a beer. "Brownies, yum."

After three hours of poker and sports talk, Jake was up $5.75.

On the way out the door, Mike said, "Jake, I hear you may be having company from Dallas this summer."

"Yeah, looks like." Jake hadn't thought he had decided. He had come tonight thinking he might talk it over with Nate, but as the words came out, he found that sometime during the week, he had accepted MaryEllen's proposal.

Thursday he showed up at the Double R and looked around for MaryEllen. It was early and she wasn't there. Half way though his cheeseburger and Sierra Nevada, he saw her talking with Duke at the bar. Duke laughed at what she had to say and handed her an iced tea. No Sierra Nevada for Jake this time. With her newly coiffed do...she must have just gotten out of Belle's Beauty Salon... on top of her crocked smile, she eased herself into Jake's booth. The smell of her hairspray reminded Jake of his mom after she had visited Belle's.

MaryEllen squeezed the lemon into her tea, added three Sweet and Lows, attempted her most angelic smile and looked into Jake's eyes.

"Why not Lou Davis?" was Jake's greeting.

"Well, he does have being African American going for him, but he's a little dull...and a lawyer."

"Got something against lawyers?"

"No, but a two month stay with the Davises wouldn't be as interesting as a two month stay on a ranch. You'd be good for him." And he'd be good for you, Mayor Jenkins added mentally though Jake would never have guessed.

"Well,"

"You're a peach, Jake. Mrs. Truwell, the social worker with the Pathway Project, Jamal and I will be at your house next Tuesday. They should be getting in around 10, 10:30. Here I brought you the paperwork. Sign here. That's your copy. You can read the Pathway mission statement and program details. See you Tuesday." And she was off in a cloud of hairspray.

Jake sat there with two bites left of his cheeseburger and a stomach that was beginning to feel quite queasy. For the second Thursday in a row, he couldn't finish his Double R cheeseburger. Glancing at the inch pile of paperwork, he thought he'd go home and go to bed early.

"Me and Scarlet O'Hara," he thought, "I'll think about it in the morning."

Jake set the stack of Pathway papers on top of the Chronicle. He had a very large mug of black coffee, no milk...after all this was serious stuff. Scrambled eggs and whole wheat toast eaten, dishes put in the dishwasher...

indeed the dishwasher was already halfway through the wash cycle. Jake scanned the first page: "new environment," "safe positive choices," "deserving youth,""experiencing new situations," "expanding horizon," pretty much what he expected. After several pages of project goals, mission statement and objectives of the program, Jake came to "Candidate for Pathway: Jamal Jackson." Here was a one page summary of the boy who would be his charge/responsibility/roommate for the next two months. He actually sounded like a pretty good kid. Lauded by his school counselors, letter of recommendation from his pastor....oh, oh, was he, Jake, going to have to go to church?....and finally a three paragraph essay by Jamal.

I've lived in Dallas all my life. In fact I've never been out of the city. I work hard to get good grades in school. I especially like math. Next year some of us, who have done well in math, will be taking a special geometry class. Some of the kids say that sounds awful, but I think it may be pretty interesting.

I live with Jacquoline Jackson. She's my grandmother. She has raised me since I was a baby. She takes really good care of me. She thinks this summer program would be good for me because it would get me away from the bad elements in our neighborhood and let me experience rural life. I would miss my Grandmother, but it would also give her a rest from the responsibility of being my guardian.

I want to see what living somewhere besides Dallas would be like. I promise to work hard to follow the Pathway guidelines and to be a responsible candidate in the Pathway Program.

Ok, the kid sounded good on paper. Come Tuesday we'll see how he measures up....and then the next two months will show how I measure up to being a summer Pathway guardian.

CHAPTER THREE

At 11:05 Tuesday morning Jake watched from his front porch as a silver Corolla pulled into his drive. Mayor Jenkins was riding shotgun. Jake grinned at how short she was, her eyes only inches above the dashboard. That must be Ms. Truwell driving. She looked to be around Jake's age, brunette and just how he imagined a social worker should look: tidy, efficient and a little haggard. MaryEllen popped out as soon as the car braked. Ms. Truwell gathered her purse and a clipboard, exited the driver's side and walked up the porch steps, hand extended.

"Good Morning, you must be Jake Litchfield. I'm Emma Truwell and this is Jamal Jackson." She quickly shook hands with Jake and then stood to the side allowing Jake his first look at his summer charge.

Jamal wore a clean yellow t-shirt (no logo as per Pathway guidelines), jeans and tennis shoes. He was about 5 foot three, well scrubbed and about as skinny a kid as Jake had ever seen.

"Hello, sir."

Jake took the hand that was offered and responded, "Hello, Jamal, Please call me Jake."

They sized each other up. Ok, I can live with this guy was the conclusion they both came to at about the same time, though Jamal held a bit of judgment in reserve. He had to be a pretty tough kid and a bit wary to stay out of his neighborhood gang and yet not have a lot of bruises and lacerations as a result of not joining when asked. His Granny did have a lot to do with that too. Just about everyone on the block owed Jacquoline Jackson a favor or two...money she "lent," food dropped off, a sofa to sleep on when the alternative was the underpass or a crack house, and she used every one of them to keep Jamal safe and unattached from the Cheranos.

"Ms. Truwell, Mayor Jenkins, Jamal, I have some lemonade here. Perhaps you'd like to sit down and have some," Jake flinched at how weirdly formal he sounded.

MaryEllen scrambled up the porch plopping into one of the chairs Jake had positioned earlier around the circular wrought iron outdoor table.

"Oh, goody. I see Rosa left you some of her ginger cakes." Rosa was the cleaning lady who came every other week. On occasion she'd leave some of her wonderful tamales or flan. She and the rest of the town seemed to know of Jamal's arrival. This was her way of saying welcome.

"Yes, ma'am." When was the last time Jake called MaryEllen "ma'am"...that would be never. Why was he so nervous?

MaryEllen ignored the formality and began to pour lemonade for all of them.

"This is very nice," said Emma Truwell glancing at the table. Perhaps in just a bit. I'd like to look at where Jamal will be staying first. Then we can talk and have something to drink."

"Yes, ma'am."

Emma Truwell gave Jake a little smile. She had experienced this kind of nervousness before and took it as a good sign. She thought this showed that he was taking summer guardianship seriously and was uncertain about how he would handle a teenager from the barrio or, perhaps, any teenager.

"You go right ahead. I'll stay here and enjoy Rosa's ginger cakes. There may or may not be some left when you get back." MaryEllen looked like an elf with crumbs clinging to her cheek, a very smug elf.

Jake gave Ms. Truwell and Jamal a quick tour of the livingroom and kitchen. Emma made several checkmarks on the first page on her clipboard. They then went down the hall to the room that would be Jamal's bedroom. It had been Jake's room growing up. He had pulled out his old plaid orange and brown bedspread his mom had bought for him over twenty-five years ago. It's so old it's probably in style again he had thought yesterday as he made the twin bed with fresh linens. There was a bookshelf in the corner and an old (probably antique by now) wooden desk under the window that his grampa had made for his dad. Jake had stocked the bookshelf with several science fiction books he had loved as a kid: Robert Heinlein's *Starship Troopers, The Cat Who Walks Through Walls;* Asimov's *Foundations* series, and *I Robot;* Poul Anderson's *Time*

Patrol; and his more recent favorite Orson Scott Card's *Pastwatch.*

He had also purchased and tucked into the closet three long sleeved plaid shirts thinking that if Jamal did any ranch work, they would come in handy.

Emma Truwell made several more check marks on her clipboard, smiled at Jamal, "It looks like you'll be quite comfortable here. What do you think?"

"Yes, ma'am. It looks real, um, very nice."

"Jamal, why don't you go out and have some cookies and lemonade with Mrs. Jenkins while I talk with Mr. Litchfield for a minute or two."

"Mr. Litchfield, shall we sit at the kitchen table?" They pulled chairs and sat opposite each other.

"Well, Mr. Litchfield, everything seems to be in order. I'll be back in a week or ten days to check on how things are going. I'll call the evening before I come."

"As you know from your documentation, there is a stipend for Jamal provided by the Dallas Rotary through Pathway Project. I've given him the first installment. These funds are for his personal use. The Project expects most everything to be provided by the host families. The participant would not be expected or required to pay for everyday incidentals."

Jake, who had not thoroughly read all the documentation and didn't know about the stipends, was shocked that Ms. Truwell seemed to think he'd ask Jamal for money. His face must have shown it...it is a wonder he ever wins at poker.

"Mr. Litchfield, I'm not insinuating that you would. There are just somethings I like to make perfectly clear. Do you have any questions for me?"

Still stinging from her money comment, Jake almost stifled what he was about to ask, but decided for the sake of 'perfect clarity' went ahead, "I thought since Jamal was coming to a ranch for a, um, rural experience, I might have him do some chores and ranch work. Would that be a problem?" He was about to add that he would pay Jamal a ranchhand's wage, but felt that made what he had planned for Jamal look like a job and not the ranch experience he had in mind.

"Are you saying you see Jamal as a ranch hand?" Even though there was no judgment in her voice, Jake felt he was being misunderstood.

"No, ma'am. Not at all. I just thought I could teach him to ride and he could come out with me to check the herd and that he could have some chores like collecting the eggs or doing the dishes."

"Mr. Litchfield that sounds fine. We want Jamal to act as part of the family and though as a single male with no children, you are not the typical host family, we view you as a good fit for Jamal. As I said I will be back to check on how things are going and, at that time, correct any misunderstandings. Now, shall we join Jamal and Mrs. Jenkins?"

Jake followed Ms. Truwell out to the porch feeling less sure of his decision to be a 'host family' than ever.

The foursome sat for twenty minutes more drinking lemonade, eating ginger cakes and making small talk. Well, Mayor Jenkins and Ms. Truwell did almost all of the talking. Then the Mayor and the social worker got into the car, waved and drove off.

"Um, more lemonade, Jamal?"

"No, thank you, sir. But I'd like to use the restroom."

"Oh, down the hall, first door on your left, past your bedroom. I'll bring in your suitcase."

"Thank you, sir. I can handle it."

Jamal picked up his small black suitcase and went inside.

"This is way too awkward," Jake thought. He gathered up the used glasses, pitcher and ginger cake dish and brought them into the kitchen. He was loading the dirty dishes into the dishwasher when Jamal came in. He closed up the dishwasher and gestured for Jamal to sit at the kitchen table.

"I think the best I can do is to tell you straight up what I'm doing and what I expect from you. I'd think things would be easiest for both of us if you tell me up front if you don't understand or if you don't want to do something or think you shouldn't or whatever."

Jamal looked a little skeptical and a little wary so Jake thought he'd be a little more specific.

"Like, I'd appreciate it if you could cut down on the 'sirs' and call me 'Jake' most of the time. Like, I'd like you to put your dishes in the dishwasher after meals and sometimes unload it. I'd like you to make your bed in the mornings. I'll show you how to collect the eggs before breakfast and then I'd like that to be a chore you do."

Jamal was looking less wary, but Jake was feeling he wasn't quite making his point.

"I got a mare, Sadie. She's a good old horse and gentle. I don't have time to ride her much anymore and I think she misses it. I'll teach you how to saddle her and ride her if you are ok with that and you can ride out with me sometimes." Jake paused. Living alone he wasn't used to long conversations.

"That sounds fine, s..., Jake. When do we start?"

"How about now? We'll get Sadie set up and then you can practice riding in the corral. I put a couple long sleeved shirts in your closet. You might think the t-shirt is cooler, but the long sleeves will protect you from the sun a whole lot better."

"Ok, Jake (the name sounded awkward, it would take time...actually one week...for it to become natural for him). I'll change and be right out." Jamal hurled himself down the hall and into his room obviously ready for a grand adventure.

To Jake having been raised on the ranch, saddling and riding was so second nature that he had to really think about the steps. He and Jamal went to the barn to get the tack. His old saddle that he had used as a kid needed some oiling and TLC. He thought about doing that first, but figured Jamal could do it after his lesson. They put the saddle, blanket and reins on the corral fence. Then walked over to the west gate. Jake whistled for Sadie. Sadie came promptly, whinied and bobbed her head.

She was the biggest animal Jamal had ever seen. He didn't want to show his nervousness, but he couldn't stop himself from taking a step back.

"That's a good old girl," Jake murmured as he rubbed her nose and patted her neck. "You need to touch to let her know what you want. You don't have to talk to her, but, well, why not. It will help you two get to know each other. If you have to go around her back, pat her before you do to let her know where you are. You don't want to startle her when you are back there."

"Ok, we start with the reins. Here you slide the bit in like this and then put the harness up and around like this." Jake demonstrated twice. "Now you try it."

Jamal tried to imitate Jake's actions, but unlike with Jake, Sadie pushed the bit with her tongue."

"She's not cooperating."

"I guess she can tell that you're new at this. Here." Jake covered Jamal's hands with his and guided the bit into place. They practiced together twice more and then Jamal tried again on his own. Sadie tried the tongue trick, but this time Jamal ignored it and slide the bit into place. A slow smile spread across his face. It was like getting an 'A' on a pop quiz in Mr. Lemon's pre-algebra class.

Jamal pulled out the bit and slide it into place again. Sadie snorted.

"I guess she figures you know what you're doing now and wants to get on with it. Ready to go for a ride?"

Jamal nodded and carefully pulled the reins over Sadie's ears as Jake instructed. Jack quickly saddled the mare giving instructions on how tight to cinch the saddle belt under her belly.

"Ah, you can use the upturned bucket or the fence as a step, but you might as well get used to climbing into the saddle without it."

It was a lot higher up than he had expected. Sadie was a gentle "old Girl" to Jake, but as big as she looked to Jamal when he was on the ground, she looked ten times bigger when he mounted.

Jamal's grin was replaced by a very serious expression. With Jake's help he quickly learned the signals to have Sadie go, stop, go right, go left. While Jamal and Sadie practiced in the corral, Jake saddled his horse, Ben.

He opened the corral gate and suggested a short ride to the south pasture. He wanted to check the pump he had out there. He used it to water his stock and it had been "gimpy" for the past three weeks. Jake held Ben back and they took a very slow ride to the south pasture engaging in a bit of small talk about the pastureland, Jake's herd and Jamal's ride from Dallas to Clayton Springs. Jake did most of the talking. Jamal half listened and responded when necessary. Most of his concentration was given to not falling off this enormous animal.

When they got there, sure enough, the pump hadn't cured itself.

"Looks like I'm going to have to break this down and see what's ailing it," Jake imagined that he sounded "just like a cowboy" to Jamal when he said that.....ailing it?..... what is wrong with me?

"You gonna do that now?"

"No, I didn't bring my tools and I need to pick up a gasket at Ace. I'll come out, oh probably Friday."

"Can I come too? And help? I'd like to learn to fix stuff."

Jake thought about saying, "Much obliged," but figured that was way over the top.

"That'd be good."

Back at the ranch as Jamal slid off Sadie, his knees came very close to buckling when his feet hit the ground.

On TV riding a horse looked easy, but he found aches in muscles he didn't even know he had. He did his best to hide it, and Jake did his best not to notice as he helped Jamal take off the riding gear and stow it in the tack area of the barn. They then wiped and brushed down their horses. Jamal was careful not to go behind Sadie and kept letting her know where he was by brushing and patting. Jake put the horses' dinner in their troughs and walked with Jamal to the house.

They hadn't really done much, but Jake could see that Jamal was exhausted.

"It's a bit early, but how about I nuke some tamales Rosa left, make a salad and call it dinner."

"Sounds good. Would it be ok if I called my Grandmother after dinner?"

"No problem. I'm sure she'd like to hear about your first day here."

Jake made enough dinner for four, but there were no leftovers. Maybe it was being outdoors most of the day, maybe it was nervousness or maybe that's just how much a thirteen year old boy ate.

After supper they cleared the table and started the dishwasher, Jake nodded to the phone.

"You call your Grandma. I'm going to my office and do some paperwork.

Jamal appreciated that Jake was giving him some privacy. He was feeling homesick....as well as really, really sore....and missed his Gran. This was the first night in thirteen years that he wouldn't be going to sleep in their tiny apartment in the Dallas barrio.

"Hi G-mama."

"Oh, Jamal, I'm so glad you called. I was just thinking of you." Of course, she was thinking of him. He hadn't left her thoughts for a moment. She missed him terribly, but this was best for him so she tried her best to hide her lonesomeness and her worry."

They talked for twenty minutes. Jamal told her all about Sadie and G-mama told him about Tiffany's amnesia. Tiffany was a character in G-mama's favorite soap.

At the end of the call, Jamal was yawning and having trouble keeping his eyes open.

"You sound just tuckered," said G-mama. "You thank Mr. Jake for your ride and supper and then why don't you go to bed?"

It was only 7, but that sounded just fine. After saying good night to his grandma, Jamal stuck his head into Jake's office.

"Is it ok if I go to bed now?"

"Sounds like a good idea. Got everything you need?"

"Maybe, toothpaste?"

"It's in the cabinet over the sink."

"Thanks. Night."

"Good night, Jamal."

Jake looked away from the computer screen to the doorway that Jamal had just vacated. It had been an awkward day getting used to each other. He imagined the stress and strangeness had exhaused the kid, plus, of course, his first experience with a horse. Jake found himself smiling. It had been kind of fun teaching him about riding and getting him acquainted with the ranch. Jamal might be a bit stiff tomorrow so he'd need to take it easy on him. Much as he wasn't fond of change, Jake thought his might turn out to be a pretty good summer.

CHAPTER FOUR

The next morning Jamal walked stiffly to the breakfast table and winced as he sat down.

"A little sore this morning?"

"I've never been this sore. Even my butt...um...rear hurts." Jamal admitted with a pained smile.

"Well, I guess that's to be expected. You'll get used to it all. In the meantime, why don't I ride out alone today and you stick around the house. You can unload the dishwasher and check the hens after breakfast. Hungry?"

"Yes, sir. Very. Sounds good. I don't think I'll ever be able to sit in that saddle again."

Jake smiled, "You'll be fine in a couple days."

And so he was. In ten days he was riding...mostly gracefully. Jake said he was a little jealous about the way Sadie took to him. Jamal smiled and said the carrots he brought her everyday probably swayed her loyalty.

A routine began to form. Mayor Jenkins brought over the Davis girls, Brenda and Vicki, who took Jamal to church and swimming at their pool a couple days a week.

Mid-June Jake and Jamal rode out to the pump and worked all morning refitting the gasket and casing, and cleaning off the rust. In the end it worked like new and Jake sincerely complimented Jamal on his help.

Jamal called his Gramma every night. He went through a spell of being seriously homesick. He didn't tell anyone, but G-mama and Jake were both aware of it and just let it run its course.

Jamal would tell his Gramma about a ride with Sadie, swimming lessons at the Davises, signing up for his Clayton Springs library card, Rosa's great meals.... "not as good as your hamburger casserole, but tasty"...and G-mama would keep him up to date on the soaps. One night after talking with his Gramma, Jamal told Jake that Tiffany was probably carrying her uncle's child though she didn't remember because of her amnesia. Jake was momentarily horrified, then he realized by watching Jamal's sly smile that Tiffany was not one of his schoolmates from Dallas.

On the Fourth of July after watching the parade through the five blocks of downtown Clayton Springs, Jake and Jamal went to the annual BBQ at Nate and Sissy's house. Jake brought a 12 pack of Big Wave (Nate's favorite) and Jamal brought tapioca pudding that he had made in the morning using his Grandmother's special recipe. She had dictated it to him over the phone the previous evening. Well, yes, it was the same recipe as was on the side of the tapioca box, but with a pinch of ginger added.

Nate met them at the door. He was holding Izzy, his youngest. At a year and a half she rotated between shy and gregarious. She had decided on gregarious today.

"Hi, hi, hi, hi, hi, hi."

"New word?" Jake asked as he handed Nate the beer and took Izzy.

"Hi, hi, hi, hi, hi, hi."

"Ya think? I hope you appreciate the fresh diaper."

"Such a domestic. Where's my other big girl?"

His other girl, Evie, was clinging shyly to her daddy's leg. She was a vision in a hello kitty (pink) t-shirt, 3 pink tutus and pink cowboy boots."

"Where's your hat?" asked Jake. She scurried to the livingroom and found her pink sequinned cowboy hat under the coffee table."

"Wow," was all Jake had to say.

"Hey, Jamal, thanks for the pudding. How're the swimming lessons coming?"

Jamal stepped inside and looked around. "Ok. Should I put this in the frig?"

It'll be fine on the table over there. Brenda, Tim, Chris and Vicki are outside if you like."

Jamal was happy to ditch both the adults and the toddlers, but Evie followed him at a distance to the backyard.

"I think she has a crush," said Nate, "How 'bout we open these?"

"Baba," said Izzy with her lower lip beginning to tremble.

"I'll get the baba; you get me a beer," said Jake as he ambled toward the kitchen jiggling Izzy.

Later Lou Davis joined the group of men hanging around the BBQ supervising Nate cooking the hotdogs, hamburgers and steaks.

"I must admit, Jake, I was a bit put out that Mayor Jenkins went to you first for Jamal's summer placement. I, well, you know, I thought my family would be a good fit."

"Well, the thought crossed my mind also," Jake replied, "but our MaryEllen works works in mysterious ways. Jamal is such a good kid. I think he'd fit in well most anywhere, and, well, he seems to enjoy the ranch and I don't mind him there."

Nate grinned, "That's high praise from our taciturn friend here. You know you're having a good time with this summer program."

Jake gave a little nod.

"Well, my girls like having him over. Did you know that he didn't know how to swim? Brenda went online looking up swimming fundamentals. She designed a regime of lessons. He has a chart with stars and everything. I told Brenda she could be a personal trainer when she grows up. But you know what she says? She tells me she would be too busy running the World Bank!" Lou beamed in the direction of his girls who were with the group of eight or so teens and pre-teens at the picnic table under the dogwood. They seemed to be all talking at once while eating huge plates of BBQ.

Jamal was sitting between Bella and Charles. Charles, a 10 year old, was pleased to be included for the first time in what he saw as the big kids, and was beaming to be sitting next to Jamal.

The topic of Jake came up and Jamal casually asked if they knew why he wasn't married.

"OMG! Don't you know?" Melinda a fifteen year old who had a well-earned reputation as a drama queen went on, "It was tragic, just tragic."

Most everyone at the table rolled their eyes but didn't interrupt.

"Jake dated Natalie Ann Turner all through high school. They were soooo much in love. Natalie was a cheerleader and Jake played all kinds of sports. Then they went to U T in San Antonia.

"Hook 'em horns," chorused from most everyone around.

Jamal looked around confused.

"Oh, it's just what you say every time your mention UT," Julie explained.

"Well, as I was saying," Melinda continued. "They were sooo much in love....meant to be together forever."

She paused for effect.

"Well?" asked Jamal who despite himself was caught up in the drama.

"After they graduated from UT.."

"Hook 'em horns."

"You rural folks are weird." commented Jamal. "Go on."

"After they graduated," Melinda sighed deeply, "Jake came back to Clayton Springs, but Natalie didn't want a small town life. She got her MBA and now works in Houston for International Oil.......now she's some bigwig in the company.....and Jake came home with a broken heart. "Melinda signed again and her eyes teared up a bit. "He never got over her."

Jamal had eaten his way through two hot dogs, a heap of potato salad and six giant strawberries during the telling of the tale. He finished his third hot dog and expressed his need for dessert.

"Me, too," said Mike, a redhead who was a year older than Jamal.

On the way to the dessert table Mike said quietly, "Just like the movies, that was loosely based on a true story."

At the dessert table Jamal packed his plate with a piece of peach pie, two brownies, a slice of red velvet cake and more strawberries. When he looked, he was pleased to see that his tapioca pudding was all gone.

With no irony in her voice, Sissy asked if he and Mike had found enough to eat.

"Yes, Ma'am," they said in unison and headed back to the "fun" table.

"What a nice kid," Sissy commented to Jan who was helping herself to seconds.

"Yeah, they are a good bunch of kids."

At 5 on the button Sissy called for the clean-up crews. She organized the men to clean up the yard and the kids to work inside. She and four other women paper plated and saran wrapped the leftovers. Jake would find enough for dinner tomorrow night in the cab of his Ford 250 when he and Jamal left for home.

As Jake was bringing in a large trash bag full of recyclable cans and bottles, he was pleased to see Jamal in the middle of the teenage clean-up crew, laughing and doing a good job of scrubbing the kitchen counter.

After the house and yard sparkled, half the party-goers left for home and the other half walked the half mile to the community center for the fireworks display. Jamal was with his group of friends in the lead. Jake walked with

Nate and Sissy. Izzy was in the stroller crowing "Walk-Walk." Evie was holding Sissy's hand wistfully watching the teenagers ahead. After they had gone a block, Izzy was fast asleep and Nate was carrying a nodding Evie.

"I can come help with the haying next Friday."

"Thanks, Nate, I appreciate that. It's a dirty, hot job."

"Wish I could help," John said coming up from behind.

"No way," said Nate.

"Not gonna happen," said Jake. Three years ago, John had attempted to help with the haying. After less than an hour, they had to call an ambulance. John had a serious asthma attack and was hospitalized for three days.

"Come around four for pizza and beer."

"Will do. I'll pick up the pizza for you."

"Is Jamal going to help?"

"Yeah, he's gonna be there. He said Brenda, Vicki and Les will be coming too. Les is a ranch kid so he knows what he's getting into. On the other hand, Brenda and Vicki...."

"They're good kids. They really like Jamal so I think they'll try. Well, Vicki will work without complaining. It's a little iffy with Brenda."

She can always sit on the fence and supervise."

"Oh, don't tell her that. She'll run us all ragged."

CHAPTER FIVE

The next day was Ms. Truwell's scheduled visit. She was coming about every ten days to check on how Jamal and Jake were doing. Jake was more comfortable around her now. She had shared with him some of the trauma she was dealing with as a mom of two pre-teens and a husband, who as a long haul truck driver, was often away.

"It's so great when he's home. He is such a sweetheart and he's great with the kids. It just makes it all the harder when he heads out a week or two at a time."

She had also shared with Jake how she had had serious misgivings about Jake being the summer guardian for Jamal. "But MaryEllen Jenkins raved about how wonderful you would be. You know. She can be very persuasive."

Didn't Jake know all about that!

She arrived mid-morning and took coffee instead of lemonade at the kitchen table. Jamal handed her a steamy mug and put the sugar and milk beside it.

"Thanks, I really, really need this. Lonny is on the road and Dwayne, the younger one, informs me last night that, oh, he has a project due today, and, oh, it was assigned at the beginning of the summer class, and, oh, there had to be a poster and a three paragraph essay, and, oh yeah, some kind of a 3 dimensional thingy to go with it all, and, oh he hadn't really started, and –get this-- he hadn't picked his topic. He had to take this summer course as a make-up for the one he flunked last semester. It's a good thing I'm not in jail today under arrest for homicide."

She looked at Jake and Jamal who had stopped in their tracks to stare at her.

"Oh, did I say all that out loud? Just let me get some of this coffee in me and I will transform into the efficient, Ms Truwell, social worker."

And she did. She took out her ubiquitous clipboard and asked Jake, then Jamal a three page list of questions. When she was done, she asked to talk with Jamal privately.

Jake said he had chores in the garden, refilled his and her coffee mugs and left through the back door.

"I wanted to give you a chance to talk to me without your summer guardian present. So, how are you two getting along?"

"Just fine, Ma'am."

"Problems?"

"No, ma'am."

"Care to elucidate?"

Jamal smiled. He liked it that Ms. Truwell used such a grown-up word with him and that she expected him to know what it meant. He was even more pleased that he did.

"Well, ma'am. I've learned to ride Sadie. I told you that last time. I help around the house and the ranch. I'm learning to swim at the Davis house. We went to a great BBQ, Fourth of July party. I helped fix the pump, and Jake said I was truly a help."

"Jamal who wasn't much of a talker suddenly looked embarrassed at the length of his response and added, "It's just fine here, ma'am.""

"No problems, at all?"

"Well, I do miss my grandmother, but Jake has me call her almost every night. It doesn't cost him anything extra. He told me he has this special phone plan. It's different from the one my gramma has. So I call her, and the long distance call doesn't cost Jake. And since I'm calling her, it doesn't cost Gramma either."

"I know you miss your gramma and I'm sure she misses you too." Emma Truwell had stopped by Jacquoline Jackson's house just last night. They talked about how she thought Jamal was doing. Jacquoline was adamant that Jamal enjoy his summer away from Dallas. No matter how much they missed each other. This was right before she came home to Dwayne and his project.

"And I'm glad you and Jake seem to be hitting it off. So no problems. Anything....uncomfortable ever happen?"

"Well."

Emma Truwell held her tongue knowing that Jamal would eventually fill the silence.

"Well, there was this one time at the Davis's house. That's where I go to learn to swim. Brenda Davis is teaching me. I started as a guppie according to her lesson plans."

"Um."

"Well, they asked me to stay for dinner. I called Jake, and he said it was ok. Actually I've eaten over there a couple times."

"Um."

"Well, Mrs. Davis served artichokes." Jamal looked at Ms. Truwell as though this explained it all.

"I'm not sure I understand."

"I felt like a real duffus. I had no idea how to eat it. I watched everybody else dip the leaves into this little bowl of butter we all had and then scrap the leaves with their teeth. That was kinda weird, but it tasted ok. When they were done with the leaves, they cut the rest of it up and drizzled the butter all over it. I didn't notice that they separated out the fuzzy part. I took an enormous bite of the fuzz. It was gross and I choked. I spit it out all over my plate."

Ms. Truwell could tell from the look on his face that Jamal had been mortified.

"What did the Davises do?"

"Mr. Davis slapped my back 'cause I choked and then they all said that it was ok and they should have told me, but I was really embarrassed. I should have known better. I spit it out right on the plate!"

"Why should you have known better, Jamal? It was a brand new experience for you. That's how we all learn. I imagine every grown-up had something similar happen to them as a kid."

"That's pretty much what Mrs. Davis said. Then she promised to have corn on the cob next time I came over," Jamal said with a little smile. "Do you really think it was ok?"

"Yes, Jamal, I do. It's hard to be in an embarrassing situation and it sounds like the Davises like having you at their house and will have you over again."

"Yeah, I'll be going back for my 'minnow' lesson on Saturday, and they'll probably ask me to stay for dinner."

"I'm really glad this is working out so well. I did have my reservations, but Clayton Springs seems to be a good fit."

"Yeah, I'll miss everybody when I do home, but I've already promised to keep in touch and, well, maybe, I mean, I haven't asked, but it things keep going well, well, maybe next summer...." Jamal trailed off but looked hopefully at Ms. Truwell.

"Oh, that isn't a part of the Pathway Project. It is just for the two months this summer. We have to give someone else the opportunity next summer."

"Oh, well, I was just hoping...."

"I understand, and it's great that this is such a success. Just enjoy the rest of your time here."

"Yes, ma'am." Jamal was disappointed. He had thought that if he were "pro-active" (a word and concept he had just run across in his required library reading) that he could start Ms. Truwell to work on his coming back next summer, but maybe he could work something else out like maybe hiring on with Jake—for room and board—as a summer ranch hand. He's already learned a lot about ranch life. Jake had said a couple times that he was a help. He'd use the rest of his time here showing that he could be a ranch hand

Emma Truwell gathered up her clipboard. She was pleased. This was her most successful pairing in the

Pathway Project. Jamal was disappointed about not coming next summer, but he was gaining so much from this experience. She had all but forgotten all about Dwayne and last night's fiasco and thought that this was why she had gone into social work.

She said good-bye to Jamal telling him she'd see him next in about two weeks, waved good-bye to Jake who was working the hula hoe around the vegetables in the garden, and was on her way.

She made it about 10 feet down the drive when her trunk popped open. She got out, gave the trunk a confused look, slammed it shut, waved again to Jake and now was once again on her way.

Driving back to Dallas, Emma listened to NPR until the pledge break came on. She switched to the All News-All Weather-All Traffic channel and thought again about Dwayne and his lack of ambition and focus. Maybe I can get Jamal and Dwayne together this fall. Maybe Jamal can inspire Dwayne to care about school. She spent the last 50 miles of her trip fantasizing about their friendship and Jamal's positive influence on her wayward son.

CHAPTER SIX

Rosa's husband Manual walked into Jake's kitchen at 7 AM.

"Hey, Manual, want some breakfast?"

"Nope, I ate at home. Coffee would be good though."

"On the counter. Help yourself."

Jamal was just finishing his breakfast. This morning he opted for ChocoPuffs. Jake had his standard: scrambled eggs, toast and coffee. He had added orange juice to his morning that's what he thought kids should have in the morning and he wanted to lead by example.

Nate and Mike showed up with Brenda, Vicki and Les.

"Do we get coffee too?" sassed Brenda.

"Milk and orange juice are in the refrigerator."

"Ok, let's get this show on the road. The men slurped the last of their coffee and gathered their gloves, hats and bandanas and walked to Manuel's flat bed and Jake's truck. Jamal, Brenda, Vicki and Les hopped into the bed of Jake's pick-up and they were off to the west pasture to start the haying.

The hay had been cut, dried and baled. Today they were collecting the bales to store in the barn. Even with the gloves to protect theirs hands and the bandanas to keep the dust out of their noses and mouths, they all suffered minor cuts and dirt sifted into eyes and mouths. Jake expected the kids to start strong and then fade fast, but they surprised him. They worked steadily tossing the bales up to the flatbed and the pick-up. When the trucks were full, they rode back to the ranch, drank gallons of water, ate a quick snack of apples and bananas and formed a human chain to stack the bales in the barn. Then it was off for a second load bandanas covering their mouths, they looked like Murietta's bandits on their way to rob a stage coach.

By one, they finished the second load. The barn was full. The rest would be stacked in the barnyard under a tarp. They all sat around the picnic table eating the sandwiches Jamal and Jake had prepared the night before. No one talked much.

By five they finished the fourth and final load. They cleaned up first at the outside hose and then at the kitchen sink. Even so dust billowed from their clothing. They scrubbed theirs hands, arms and faces and then devoured the twelve pizzas John brought over.

"Sorry I missed all the fun."

"Well, we appreciate the pies."

Jamal and the other teenagers ate in silence too tired to talk. The men chatted about the number of bales and how this was a better year than last. They guessed about the winter and when Jake would have to start removing the hay for feed.

"According to the almanac, we're supposed to have more than average rain this fall and the cattle should be able to pasture until December."

"Fingers crossed."

"The kids surprised me," Manual said quietly as he pulled a third soda from Jake's refrigerator, "especially those Davis girls."

"I think they wanted to keep up with Jamal." Jake was proud of his charge. "They all were pretty impressive."

John said he would take the Davis girls and Les to their homes. Everyone said a weary good night.

The hot showers felt really good. Their beds felt better. The pizza fixings would be tidied in the morning.

CHAPTER SEVEN

The next morning Jake let Jamal sleep in. He put the beer and soda cans and the pizza boxes into recycle, wiped down the counter tops and kitchen table and brewed himself a large pot of coffee.

"I'm getting old," he thought as he stretched his sore arms, legs and back.

"Morning," Jamal walked into the kitchen looking a bit like a zombie himself.

"Morning. Eggs?"

"Nope, I'm going for ChocoPuffs."

"That stuff is nasty."

"Yeah, but it tastes good and I put milk on it. Milk is good for you. And the box says I get 1/3 of my daily requirement of riboflavin."

The smiled at each other and ate the rest of their breakfasts in compatible silence.

"You going to swim lesson today?" Jake asked as he put his dishes in the dishwasher.

"Yeah, if that's ok."

"Jake had noticed that Jamal seemed to be trying too hard lately. He couldn't figure Jamal's motivation. They got along great. He hadn't a clue that Jamal was trying to think of a way to ask if he could come back next summer and wanted Jake to have no reason to say no.

"Sure, fine with me. I'm going to check the south fences and then go into town. I'll take the truck."

"You want me to come along?"

"Look, you did more than your share yesterday. Besides, don't you want to be a dolphin?"

"I have to pass minnow first and then plan on going straight to orca."

"What does Brenda say?"

"She says I have to be a triggerfish first."

"Better than a crab."

"True."

"You staying there for dinner?"

"Yeah, Mrs. Davis is cooking...."

"Fish?"

"Sloppy Joes."

Jamal slurped up a second bowl of ChocoPuffs as he watched Jake take off in the Ford to check the fences. Maybe he would wash the truck tomorrow. He stowed his dishes in the dishwasher, grabbed two carrots from the frig and went out to say good morning to Sadie and then muck her stall.

"Hey girl, how you doing? Sorry no ride today. I'll put you in the corral while I clean up your place." Jamal gave her a carrot, led her to the corral, gave her the second one and secured the gate.

He grabbed the pitchfork and wheel barrel and began to clean her stall.

"Jamal." He thought he heard someone whisper his name. He looked around. Nothing. No one. He piled some more dirty straw into the wheel barrel.

"J-dawg." This time he was sure he heard it.

Who's there?"

"Jamal, it's me." The voice came from the loft which was full of bales of hay from yesterday.

Jamal thought he recognized the voice, "Devon? D-dawg?"

"Yeah, up here." Jamal slowly climbed the ladder to the loft. He hadn't seen Devon in almost a year. They had been good friends in elementary school, but Devin had lots of trouble in class. He'd been held back a couple times and by the time they were in middle school, Devin rarely attended class.

When he got to the top of the ladder, he called again, "Devon?"

"Here."

Jamal looked over. Devon, at least he thought it was Devon, lay to the right of the ladder where a bale or two had been shoved to the side to make a small niche.

"What happened to you?" Devon's face was bruised. One eye was swollen shut. His t-shirt and pants were torn, dirty and bloody.

"I thought I'd visit you out in the country," Devon tried to joke.

"Seriously, man. What happened?"

"You know that group that you and your g-mama worked so hard to keep away from?"

"The Cheranos?"

"Yeah, I guess they decided they needed a new gay member.

"What, you're gay?"

"Yeah, but you ain't my type." This last banter had been standard between Devon and Jamal when they were friends in elementary school. Devon never 'came out.' He just always was.

Devon coughed, winced and went on, "They decided on an initiation beatdown." This was not all that unusual. Actually the beatdown could be better than some of the other initiation rituals. "But then right before they left me in the bushes at Dunsby Park, they let me know that this was just step one. After saying this and walking away laughing, I heard Bulldog mention bringing his knife tomorrow and deciding between fingers, toes or ears as a souvenir."

"So I decided I needed to get out of town. I was gonna hop a freight to California." Jamal knew Devon had no clue as to how to 'hop a freight. "I walked...ok limped by your G-mama's and saw that social worker lady go into her place. She left her car unlocked. Maybe you should tell her she needs to lock up in that part of town." Devon made jokes at anything at any time. He hadn't changed.

"I popped the trunk and climbed in. I guess I fell asleep. A little later the social worker lady got in and drove home, I guess. She didn't stay home long. She and her kid came out. She was on his case about some school thing.

They drove to Walmart. I peeked out of the trunk after they stopped, but there were too many people around for me to get out. When they came back, they didn't put anything they got into the trunk so they didn't see me. She had cooled down a bit, and they talked about a diarama – remember like those things Mrs. Brooks had us do in second grade? After they got home, I waited until I was sure they were inside for good. I was gonna leave. You know, find a freight yard..."

"Train station?"

"Yeah, whatever. Anyhow I fell asleep again and when I woke up she was driving again. Man, I really had to pee, but I held it. It took forever, man, but when she stopped and went inside, I got out. I peed in your bushes, sorry man, and then I hid under your porch. Good thing you don't have a dog, though dogs like me so I'd probably be ok."

"You've been here since Tuesday!?!"

"Yeah, mostly I stayed up here in the barn, but yesterday I was in the kitchen having one of those sandwiches when you all came back and started putting that hay in the barn. I went back under the house until about midnight when I came back up here. I just need a little time to get better and then I'm off to California."

"You hungry?"

"Yeah, I guess and really, really thirsty."

"You want to come down to the kitchen. Jake isn't home."

"Yeah, I saw him leave. I'm not sure about moving though. It was the most I could do to get up here. I think I've got some broken ribs and my arm really hurts."

"Ok, I'll go get you something."

"Come back fast. I might get bored and leave."

Jamal scrambled down the loft ladder and ran to the kitchen. Food was the easy part. He nuked several pieces of the leftover pizza and grabbed three water bottles. He pulled a couple rags from the rag box in the linen closet dampened one, found a bucket by the garden stuffed everything inside it and was back in less than five minutes.

"J-dawg, you're the best!" Devon quickly drank one bottle of water and just about finished the second when he started on the pizza. Jamal expected him to devour everything, but Devon stopped at the first piece. He laid back and closed his eyes, his face a picture of pain.

Jamal thought he had fallen asleep when he said, "Just a couple days, then I'm off to California."

Jamal took the damp rag and started to clean some of the blood from his face and shoulders. "When Jake gets back, he'll take you to the clinic."

"No."

"But look at you. You really need some help."

"You know what will happen if you get grown-ups involved." Grown-ups would mean authorities like CPS. Devon would be sent back to Dallas.

"What about your aunt?" Devon had been living with his aunt since his mom OD-ed.

"She's got a new boyfriend who doesn't want kids around. Just a couple days, man, then I'll be out of your hair.....California. Don't tell nobody." And he was asleep.

Jamal stared at him not having a clue as to what to do. After a bit, he took the empty water bottles, refilled them and left them beside a sleeping Devon. He climbed down, finished mucking Sadie's stall, checked on Devon again, still asleep, and mucked Ben's stall, laid down clean straw, wheel barreled the dirty stuff to the compost pile. His mind was alternately whirling with possibilities and blank. He collected the eggs and fed the chickens. This time when he check on Devon, he was awake. He'd drunk another bottle of water but had left the pizza alone.

"Much better."

"You don't look much better."

"Couple days. I'll be ready to go. Got any Tylenol?"

"Of course," Jamal ran to the medicine cabinet, grabbed a bottle of Tylenol Extra Strength and was back up with Devon. Devon took a couple pills with some more water wincing as he did so.

"You can use the bucket for a restroom," said Jamal.

"Gross."

"Can you make it down the ladder?"

"Not just yet. Bucket will do. Thanks."

"I need to call the Davises to tell them I'm not coming. I'll be right back."

"No."

"No, what?"

"Don't call them. Just go on as though nothing's happened that way no one will get suspicious."

"I can't just leave you here."

"Go. I'm just gonna sleep. Be normal and don't tell no one."

"Jamal looked at Devon. He felt helpless. "Can I get you anything else?"

"No, just go. Thanks J-dawg."

Jamal climbed down the ladder feeling like he was 100 years old. He got on the bike that Jake had fixed up for him and rode to the Davises without a clue as to what he would do, but feeling that his world had just collapsed.

CHAPTER EIGHT

It took Brenda exactly seventeen minutes to get the story out of Jamal. He had not planned on telling, but there he was in the shallow end relating the entire tale.

"What are we gonna do?" asked Vicki.

"We're going to keep him hidden until he's better and then we'll figure something out," Brenda said decisively. "He can't go back to Dallas, and California? Forget it. I'm going to google broken ribs and broken arms, and figure out how to deal with that. We'll get together after church tomorrow."

Somehow Jamal made it through the afternoon and Mrs. Davis's sloppy joes. Jamal wanted to bike home, but Mrs. Davis insisted that Mr. Davis put his bike in the back of her pick-up and drive him home. Mr. Davis asked about his "summer experience" on the way. The best Jamal could do was one syllable answers. They arrived the same time as Jake. Jamal thanked Mr. Davis for his ride and helped Jake with the groceries he'd gotten in town.

"Have a good lesson?"

"Yeah."

"Are you a trout?"

"I haven't passed minnow yet."

Jamal seemed down. Jake wondered if he and the Davis girls had a disagreement or if something went wrong at their house. "Everything ok?"

"Sure, fine," Jamal said with a false smile.

"Um, why don't you give your gramma a call before you go to bed?"

"Ok. I wanna say good night to Sadie."

"Why don't you call your gramma first so that it doesn't get too late for her. Take a carrot for Ben too so he won't feel left out."

Jake received a monotone "Sure" in response. What was wrong with that kid?

Jamal called his gramma and pretended that everything was normal. He asked if everything was good at home thinking that she might have heard through the barrio grapevine about Devon and would tell him the news from that end. Instead she talked about her neighbor in the next door apartment, Mrs. Gonzales, who was having problems with her hot water heater. He got off the phone as quickly as he could, grabbed carrots for the horses and went outside. Sadie was still in the corral so he put her in her stall, gave her dinner and her carrot and checked on Devon. He had eaten a little and drank all of his water.

"I used the pail. Sorry. It's gross."

"No big deal. I'll take care of it". He grabbed the pail and a couple of the water bottles. He shoved the water bottles in his shirt so that he could hold the pail in one hand and the ladder in the other. He dumped the bucket out in the compost pile and rinsed it with the garden hose.

After using the hose to fill the water bottles, he rushed back up to Devon.

"How are you doing?"

"I'm good. Much better than earlier. You'd better go back...act normal..see you tomorrow."

Jamal looked a Devon. He didn't look good.

"Go."

"See you tomorrow."

Thanks, J-dawg."

Jamal rushed back to the house and then slowed down. "Act normal," he said to himself. Said good night to Jake who was putting the last of the groceries away, and then went to bed to toss and turn all night, his mind reeling.

"Jamal, Jamal." Jamal swam up from the pull of sleep

"Jamal, it's 9:30. Mrs. Jenkins and the girls will be here really soon. Are you sick? Do you want me to call and say you're not going to church? Are you OK?"

Jamal looked around. He thought he hadn't slept at all. The last time he checked his clock, it was 5:15.

"Oh, um" Act normal he thought. He looked at Jake who was frowning a bit looking hard at him. "I just...um... no, I'm coming. I'll be ready in time."

"You sure?"

"Um"

Jamal raced to dress in his church clothes. He skipped the shower, no time, and would skip breakfast too.

He was out on the porch in fifteen minutes when MaryEllen and the Davis girls arrived.

"Hey, Jamal, how are things?" Vicki asked pointedly.

"Cool, fine." Jamal got into the back seat. He was so buzzy from lack of sleep, he forgot to say hello to Mayor Jenkins. Vicki and Brenda tried to find out about Devon through pointed glances and nudges, but Jamal ignored them. He got through the service and the after service meet-and-greet. Usually he enjoyed chatting with everyone and liked the cookies. Today he went into the bathroom to avoid everyone especially Brenda and Vicki. He just didn't have the energy. Mr. Davis found him and said they were ready to go home. He would be giving him a ride.

On the way home, Mr. Davis was oblivious to the tension among the kids in the backseat, but Mrs. Davis noticed. She thought she'd ask Vicki about it later knowing she'd be stonewalled by Brenda.

As soon as he got home, Jamal grabbed a couple carrots and ran to the barn.

"Devon?"

"Here."

"I told Brenda and Vicki about you."

"What? Why did you do that?"

"Brenda just got it out of me. They're cool. They can help you get down the loft ladder so you can come inside. Brenda looked up some stuff on the internet. She says she'll bind your ribs and 'stabilize your arm' I think...."

"Jamal." Jake was calling from the back door. "Jamal."

"Gotta go. I'll be back with something to eat." Jamal scrambled down the ladder and ran to the house.

"Hey"

"Why don't you make yourself a sandwich. I bought cheese, ham and turkey yesterday."

"Yeah, great. I'm really hungry. I'll make, uh, three. Is that ok?"

"Sure. You're a growing boy and I think you need more than riboflavin." Jake smiled, but Jamal seemed to miss the joke.

"I've already eaten. After I pay a couple bills, I'm taking Ben for a Sunday ride. What to come?"

"Um, maybe."

Jamal went to the refrigerator to get the sandwich fixings. Jake stared hard at his back. "Maybe he is still tired from all the work he did Friday," he thought. Out loud he said, "Put some vegetables on those sandwiches." Jeez, he sounded like a mom.

Jamal made the three turkey sandwiches with lettuce, tomato, pickles. He took them with a gallon of milk and two glasses to the barn. Jake's office window faced front so he gambled on doing this unseen.

"Hey"

"Hey"

"I brought sandwiches."

"Great I'm hungry." Devon must have been feeling better because he quickly downed two of the sandwiches and a big glass of milk."

"So, how was church?"

"Well, you know, fine, I guess."

"Look, I'm really much better, really. I think in just a couple days I'll be off and you won't have to worry about me any more."

And what would happen to Devon when he was 'off,' Jamal shuddered to think about it.

"So what are you doing this afternoon?"

"Jake wants to go for a ride."

"Um, truck or horse?"

"Horse."

"Dude, you are so country. Who da thought? This I gotta see...J-dawg on a real live horse. Do you lasso too?"

"I didn't tell Jake I'd go."

"You gotta go, man. First of all, I really need to see you on a horse," Devon grinned (well, half grinned since half of his face was swollen and couldn't move), "And you gotta act normal. I think I can handle the ladder today. You go and I'll come down and maybe wash off and stuff."

"You really think you can handle it?"

"Yeah. You better go now and take the milk with you."

Back in the kitchen Jamal cleaned up and put lunch things away. He walked down to Jake's office.

"Jake?"

"Yes?"

"A ride would be fine. I'll get Sadie ready. How about I get Ben ready too?" Jamal didn't want Jake to spend too much time in the barn.

No, you just take care of Sadie. I'll be out in about 10 minutes. Leave Ben to me." Jake appreciated the offer, but thought Ben was a little too spirited. He might object to Jamal trying to saddle him.

The phone rang and Jake picked up the office extension. It was Brenda.

"I'll take it in the kitchen."

"Hello." Both Jamal and Brenda waited for the click of Jake hanging up his end.

"We can't come today." Jamal had been so out of it during church he hadn't caught Brenda saying that she and Vicki would try to come over.

"Ok"

"We have to go to my aunt's house for some sort of family thing. But we'll come tomorrow. I got all kinds of information from the net about treating wounds." Now Brenda was whispering, "Gotta go. Here comes mom."

Jamal walked to the barn. He talked to Sadie as he put on the reins and saddle. She looked at him a little disappointed that he came without carrots.

"Well, girl," he said loud enough for Devon to hear, "We're going for a little ride. Jake is coming right out to get Ben and then we'll be gone for about an hour."

"You're looking like a real ranch hand," Jake said as he entered the barn. Two days ago Jamal would be on top of the world because of that compliment. Now it hardly registered. All he could think about was leaving the barn quickly so Devon wouldn't be discovered.

Their ride was mostly silent. Jake tried to engage Jamal in conversation. Jamal was trying so hard to act "normal" and not appear suspicious, he could find nothing to say. Finally Jake gave up and figuring that teenagers could be moody. He just hoped that this mood changed soon.

When they got back Jamal looked everywhere for evidence that Devon had been inside. He noticed that some of the orange juice was gone and the towel in his bathroom as damp, but nothing else was amiss. Jake would never guess that someone had been in the house.

CHAPTER NINE

On Monday Jake took off with Manual to move the herd to another pasture just before Brenda and Vicki biked over.

"Hi, Jamal, where's Jake?"

"He's gone off with Manual. He said he'd be gone 'til dinner."

"Ok then, let's get Devon."

"What's all that stuff?" Jamal asked as he ran to catch up with Brenda.

"Stuff to fix him up. Let's go."

She climbed the ladder calling, "Devon, I'm Brenda, Jamal's friend. I'm gonna help you."

Brenda was a take-charge person. She had Devon down the ladder and at the kitchen table in no time.

"Take off you shirt."

Giving Devon no time to object or to feel embarrassed, Brenda whipped his shirt off and began to swab his cuts with hydrogen peroxide. She wrapped his ribs with a long cotton gauze strip she bought at CVS. "This really won't help much. They'll just heal on their own, but it will make you feel better. Ok, your arm, does it feel better holding it close or out from your body?"

"Close."

"Then it's probably broken, not dislocated." This information she remembered from a survival show she and her dad watched. The guy in the show held his arm away from his body. It was dislocated. His friend had to put it back in place by having him hold a bucket filled with rocks over a log. At least she sort of remember that. She had been little and had closed her eyes during that part only hearing the narrative. She was very glad Devon's arm didn't have dislocation symptoms.

"We'll use these to make a cast." She pulled duct tape and plastic hangers from the CVS bag.

Jamal tried to imagine how hangers and duct tape could make a cast. He couldn't figure how it could possibly work.

"Jamal, get something to cut this plastic hanger." Jamal went to Jake's workshop area in the garage and brought back a tool that looked like heavy duty scissors. Brenda directed Jamal to cut the hangers so she could use the long plastic bottom pieces.

"Make them about 10 inches long. I'll need, oh, maybe eight of them." She told Vicki to cut the duct tape in lengths of about 10 inches also.

"I don't know how many I'm going to use so just keep cutting. Hang them from the side of the table like this. She demonstrated sticking the top inch of the tape to the edge of the table.

Mr. Davis loved an old TV show called Macgyver. Macgyver was always using duct tape to get out of a do-or-die situation. On occasion Vicki and Brenda would keep their dad company during the show. Wouldn't he be surprised at how Brenda was 'doing a Macgyver'....not that he would ever find out.

Brenda sent Jamal back to the workshop for a measuring tape. She then used the tape to measure around Devon's arm: 7 ½ inches on average, smaller at the wrist and larger by the elbow. She took five of the duct tape strips and lined them up side by side, sticky side up. Then she put six of the plastic rods across the top of the tape. Several times the tape shifted so she had Vicki and Jamal hold down the ends of the tape while she repositioned the rods. When they were fairly well lined up, she carefully put three more tape strips crosswise.

"Ok, let's give this a try." She flipped the tape/rod concoction over and had Devon put his arm on top going the same direction as the rods. Gently she pulled it around so that it encircled his arm. "It shouldn't be loose, but it shouldn't be tight either. How does that feel?"

"Uh, good?"

"Good." She secured it with several more strips of duct tape and then took the roll and wound it round and round until Devon had a silver cast. "I put tape around the ends so the rods won't poke you. I wish I would have thought of padding it with gauze first. If it bothers you, we can redo it."

`She used more hydrogen peroxide to clean Devon's face. Found Neosporin in her bag and smeared it every where.

"Jamal, do you have some clean clothes for him. I think what he's wearing should be burned."

"Girl, you have no sense of fashion," quipped Devon as he posed tying to look like a *Cosmo* model. He simply looked grotesque, but everyone was too polite to say so.

"Yeah."

"Something comfortable...like sweats"

"Sweats! I just don't think I can sink that low, and I'd be so disappointed if my man Jamal owned any sweats."

It was good that Devon was obviously feeling better and comfortable with Brenda and Vicki, but they ignored him anyway.

Jamal got him some clean underwear, a t-shirt and a pair of pajama bottoms. Devon said he was ready for the cover of *Ebony: Casual Elegance*. When Jamal went to toss the old clothes in the kitchen trash, Vicki grabbed them and said they would toss them on their way home. Jamal cringed. If Jake had seen them, the cat would be out of the bag as his gramma would say.

They tidied all evidence of medical proceedings into Brenda's bag and spent the rest of the afternoon like regular teenager just hanging: eating talking, joking. It felt really good until they looked at clock and figured they'd better get Devon hidden away.

Brenda and Vicki left. Jamal looked around at the kitchen. It looked good. He put away the tools he'd gotten from the garage and tried to read a library book, one of the required summer reading books from school, but couldn't concentrate. He tried writing in his journal, a requirement for the Pathway Project, but what he wrote sounded stilted. After all it was a lie.

Finally he thought he'd get dinner ready for Jake. He made a big salad (vegetables are good), shucked some corn for corn-on-the-cob, molded some hamburgers into patties and poured Pork 'n Beans out of the can and into a saucepan ready to cook on the stove.

When Jake came home, he was pleased with Jamal's effort with dinner. He hoped that this indicated the end of the moodiness, but Jamal continued to be edgy and tense throughout dinner.

"Kids, teenagers, who can understand them?" He was glad Brenda and Vicki had come over. Jamal seemed to enjoy being with them, but he just couldn't get back to the easy relationship he'd had with Jamal, when was it, just last week? Had he done something? Had Jamel done something? He supposed he'd finally have something of interest for Emma Truwell's checklist if this continued until her next visit.

By Wednesday they weren't speaking much at all to each other. Jake decided to give Jamal his space. Jamal felt so guilty that he avoided Jake. Wednesday night Jamal made his regular call to his grandmother. Devon was talking about leaving Saturday. He was going to catch a freight. He even had Jamal look up train schedules. It made no sense, but Jamal didn't have a better plan.

As usual, Jamal called his grandmother after dinner. G-mama didn't want to talk about her soap operas. Instead, she immediately said, "Ok, Jamal. I've had enough of this. You had better tell me what is going on."

"What do you mean? Everything's fine. Jake's fine. I'm, uh, eating good. Church."

"Stop that right this minute. I know you. I changed your diapers and have watched you and watched out for you every day of your life. What the hell is wrong?"

"Yikes, G-mama never, I mean never swore...and she would wash out my mouth and be disappointed with me for a week if I ever said 'hell' to her!" thought Jamel. What was he going to do?"

"Is it Mr. Jake? Has he done something to you?"

"Oh, no, no, no G-mama. Jake, he's fine. He's a really good guy. He'd never.."

"Then you had better tell me right now." His gramma had calmed down a bit, but Jamal could hear the love and concern in her voice. He also heard the tone that would tolerate nothing but the truth.

Still he tried, "It's noth...." for a half second then, "I, I'm so sorry, G-mama," and he told her everything. It was both a relief and a burden to have told. Jamal was almost sick from emotion. His grandmother, however, was very calm and direct.

"Ok, Jamal. You've done mostly right. Now we have to make it the rest of the way right. Please ask Jake to come to the phone." Jamal felt his stomach twist.

"You're gonna tell him?" It wasn't really a question, but G-mama took it as one.

"No, Jamal, you are. I'm just going to let him know that you are going to talk to him and that I will support whatever he decides to do."

He thought things couldn't get worse, but here he was at the bottom of a dark, dark pit. He wanted to run away but barely had the energy to go get Jake to talk with G-mama.

"Evening, Ms. Jacquoline."

"Good evening, Mr. Jake. I'll get right to it. Jamal is a good boy, but we need to remember he is still just a boy, and, well, good intentions are not always sufficient. He will be telling you what he has been doing and you have my full support with whatever you do as a result of what he tells you. You and I have only talked a bit on the phone, but from what Jamal has had to say about you and from our conversations, I can tell that you are a good man who will do the right thing. I'd appreciate a call tomorrow."

Jake had no idea that he was parroting G'mama's earlier comment when he hung up the phone and said, "What the hell is going on?"

He took one step toward the kitchen table where Jamal was sitting looking as if his world was falling apart when the phone rang. Jake just stared at it for a full ring, took a breathe—some of his natural humor returning-thought "Probably some guy wanting to sell me solar." But it wasn't.

"Er, hello Gwen. Ah, now's not a good time...but I... you really need... What (he skipped 'the hell' this time) is going on?....fine. I'll put the porch light on."

He hung up the phone again. Bluster gone, confusion reigning.

"Ok, Jamal, there is something big happening and I seem to be one of the few people in the state that doesn't know what is happening. Your grandmother tells me you have something to tell me. The Davises, that was them on the phone, are on their way over—all of them—to have a talk. Ok, Jamal, spill it."

CHAPTER TEN

Jamal talked for the twenty minutes it took the Davises to arrive. Not once could he look Jake in the eye. He did his best to give Jake the facts and no excuses. He finished and said, "I'm sorry, Jake, really sorry."

Jake had just enough time to get a pot of coffee brewing when the doorbell rang.

"Ok, stay right here. Do not go out to the barn." Jake answered the front door and ushered the Davises to the kitchen. When Jamal looked at Brenda, she lacked her usual confident swagger. In fact she looked like a little girl who had been caught being naughty. There was also some animosity between her and Vicki. Vicki, on the other hand, looked as though she had usurped Brenda's typical bravado.

"Jamal just told me all about Devon and what these kids have been up to. I assume that's why you are here."

"Yes," Mrs. Davis was taking point. Mr. Davis was observing. "We just found out about what's been going on. I knew something was wrong for a bit now, but it took a while to get to the truth.

Brenda glared at Vicki, but Vicki appeared not to notice nor care. Instead she seemed....focused.

"Should I go get Devon?" Jamal started to get up from the table. It was a very hard thing to do.

"No, he'll bolt." Mrs. Davis pulled a flashlight from her purse. "You all stay here. I'll get him."

It took her fifteen minutes to coax him down. Meanwhile in the kitchen Jake and Lou Davis sipped coffee. No one spoke.

"Here we are. Jake, this is Devon. Devon, I guess you know everyone else, Oh, and my husband, Brenda and Vicki's father, Lou Davis."

Devon could not find his voice. He wanted so much to run away, but this lady had a strong grip around his shoulders.

"Devon, you are not spending another night in a barn loft. We are taking you home and..."

"We are?" Lou looked a bit startled.

"You have mentioned repeatedly our spare room and how it could have accommodated a summer guest." Mrs. Davis looked pointedly at her husband. "It looks like we have one." Lou Davis looked sheepish. He had been called out.

"Yes, but legally..."

"Daddy," Vicki batted her big brown eyes at her father. "I've been thinking about that and I have a possible solution." Vicki, the quiet one, Vicki the one who always let her older sister decide what they should do and how they should do it had the floor and the kitchen was silent. She started by walking over to the side of the table where the adults were seated. In a clear strong voice she presented her case as if she were in front of the nine supreme court justices. Mostly she looked at her father, but occasionally glanced a Jake.

Did they know that Devon was 15, nearly 16? Did they know that he was really good with animals and could probably get a parttime job with Lou Anderson, the vet? Did they know that no one would object to him becoming an emancipated minor if his paperwork were presented in court by an esteemed lawyer (flattery though blatant often works wonders) and a Dallas social worker? "Devon could live with us while he goes to school or gets his GED. I could tutor him. Daddy could talk to Les Anderson and get him a sort of internship. Mr. Litchfield, maybe you could call Ms. Truwell?" Vicki took her time to make direct eye contact with each of the adults in the room. It was almost as if she said 'Ladies and Gentlemen, I rest my case.'

Everyone in the room was stunned, well, everyone except Mrs. Davis and Vicki. Mrs. Davis was not at all surprised to hear her younger daughter analyze the situation and come up with a very logical, very grown-up solution.

"How do you know that Devon's almost 16?"

"He told me and he told me that he's been pretty much on his own for a couple years. That's what made me think about emancipation, that, and hearing about some of Daddy's work." That girl could work her father. Everybody turned toward Lou. He looked both put out and proud.

"We", um, well." Lou looked at his wife and after moments of silent communication, he continued, "This is certainly a lot to think about."

"And?" said Mrs. Davis.

"And perhaps Devon can come home with us tonight. Gwen and I will talk it over. I'll do some legal research and we'll see. Ok Gwen, girls, Devon?"

Mrs. Davis still had her arm around Devon's shoulders. "You are looking a little rough, but actually like you are on the mend. Technically-yes, the letter of the law—would probably have us taking you immediately to the ER, but I think you are more in need of time to adjust. We'll go see the girls' pediatrician tomorrow."

Devon looked more than a little rough. He looked terrified. He gave Jamal a pleading look. Jamal looked at Jake, but Jake shook his head 'no.'

"All right then, shall we go?" It wasn't really a question. "We'll call you tomorrow and let you know how things have progressed." Gwen Davis, arm still firmly around Devon, led her family to the door.

She and Lou talked late into the night. Every time the guest room door opened, she called out, "Need anything, hon?" There was no escaping.

Jamal, on the other hand, was all talked out. He staggered off to his room after asking Jake if it was ok if he went to bed now. He collapsed on the top of his covers and slept until morning wearing the same clothes he had the day before.

Jake watched Jamal stagger to his room. He was oddly relieved. This scenerio wasn't anything he could have imagined, but finally it all made sense. Jamal had kept things from him, but he was a kid, and while what he did was dumb, in Jake's opinion, it was well intended, just like Ms Jacquoline said. Ah, Ms Jacquoline. Even though it was late, he decided to call, and she answered in the middle of the first ring. She was pleased that the Davises were involved, "You seem to have some good people over in Clayton Springs."

Jake told her he would keep her updated on what was happening.

"And you don't have to tell me not to mention this to anyone around here." Actually it had crossed Jake's mind, but he hadn't figured out how to bring it up. His estimation of Ms. Jacquoline went up several notches even though it was already over the moon. He said good night, finished the dregs in his coffee cup and went to bed.

CHAPTER ELEVEN

When Jamal awoke the next morning, he heard Jake in the kitchen fixing breakfast. He wondered if he would send him back to Dallas; then he felt guilty about worrying about himself and wondered what today would bring for Devon. Then he thought again about Jake sending him home and how disappointed G-mama would be. Then his head began to hurt so he decided not to think about anything. He took a short, but very hot shower, put on fresh clothes and went to the kitchen to face the morning and Jake.

"Morning."

"Morning. I fixed you a real breakfast. You need something healthy in your stomach for today."

"Yes, sir," Jake apparently wasn't wasting any time sending him on his way.

"I called Ms. Truwell. She's on her way."

"Yes, sir." Jake supposed all those 'sirs' were because Jake was feeling contrite. Well, that was a good thing!

"I'll get packed up right after breakfast."

Jake was just dishing out some perfectly scrambled eggs. He had been mentally complimenting himself on their fluffiness so Jamal's comment took a moment to register.

"Pack?"

A tiny spark of hope kindled with that question. "Yes, aren't you sending me back to Dallas?"

"Why on God's green earth would I do that?"

"Well, because, um, of all this."

They seemed to be back to day one. Jake remembered how he had decided to be completely direct with Jamal when he first arrived. It really was a lot of work raising – whoa—wait a minute—he wasn't raising –being responsible for a teenager. He knew "responsible" wasn't quite right either, but, well, moving on...

"First of all, you are staying right here. Yes, I am disappointed that you didn't tell me, but, well, I understand. The reason I think you need extra fortification this morning is that Ms. Truwell will be over to hear your story. Yes, you have to tell the whole thing again.

"I don't know how it is going to fit into the Pathway Project guidelines, but she knows you and I have developed a pretty good relationship (this made Jamal perk up considerably) and she thinks your stay here has been a 'Pathway' success story. She wants to keep it looking that way, but I made it clear that we didn't want to sacrifice Devon in the process. Agreed?"

"Yes, sir!"

Ms. Truwell stopped first at Jake and Jamal's. Jamal told her everything, but to his surprise, she just listened.

She wrote nothing down. Her clipboard and checklists were nowhere to be seen.

Her next stop was the Davis house. She told Jake and Jamal not to come. That made them a little nervous at first, but she explained the necessity of confidentiality with Devon.

The Davises, especially Lou, astonished Jake and Jamal over the next several days. He drew up the papers for Devon's 'Emancipation of a Minor.' Nothing unusual about that. However, he had a lawyer friend from a Houston firm present it to the court in Dallas so that it would look to anyone who took notice that Devon was in Houston. When the court mediator asked about Devon being able to support himself a story was presented about Devon being considered for a contract to be a hand model.

Jake thought that was about the weirdest idea ever, "You mean somebody who holds stuff for sale and you only see the hands? Who is going to believe that?"

"Exactly," Lou replied and told Jake how it was an idea he had been playing with for a part of a crime novel he was writing. "No body believes it, but it makes them think that he is in Houston doing something else—something perhaps secret if not illegal. If the Cheranos do go looking for Devon, they'll be looking into Houston's underworld, not squeaky clean Clayton Springs.

Another very useful item Lou found in his research for the court papers was Devon's birth certificate. He would be 16 in December, that they knew. What they didn't know was that the name on his birth certificate was Darwin not Devon. This was a total surprise to Devon, but it would allow him to register for school as Darwin, again making it harder for the Cheranos to track him down if they ever tried.

With the Houston lawyer, Ms. Truwell's help and no objections in Dallas whatsoever, Devon/Darwin was emancipated in record time.

"He'll be staying with us," Lou told Jake and Jamal. I know we have a couple problems to work out, but I'm surprised at how well he fits into the family."

"Problems, like him being gay?" Jamal said somewhat defensively.

"Oh, no. This biggest problem I see is that he is a Ranger fan, but I can be very persuasive, after all, I am a lawyer. He'll be wearing Dodger colors by the end of the summer." Who knew that Lou and Devon would immediately bond over baseball? Currently Lou was showing reruns of Yareil Puig's magnificent right field catch. Devon's counter was that as soon as Soto got off the disabled list the Rangers would be back on track for the pennant.

A new normal set in. Jamal and Jake gradually worked themselves back to the the easy, comfortable relationship they had before the Devon incident. Jake, much to Devon's delight –it was fodder for endless joshing—was teaching Jamal to lasso. Jamal passed minnow and was on is way to acing Stingray. Devon would watch the lessons from the side of the pool. With his new (non-duct tape) cast, he couldn't go in. On occasion Jake would join them for an after lesson dinner.

Summer was winding down. Jamal was looking forward to seeing his gramma and taking some of the advanced courses at Dallas North Town Middle School, but he would miss Jake and Brenda and Devon and Vicki and...there were so many people in Clayton Springs that he would miss. He had tentatively brought up coming back next summer to Jake. It took Jake about 5 seconds to consider and then say he thought that it was a great idea.

It was getting very close to the end of his Pathway Project stay, Jamal was in the middle of being tested to pass Stringray. He had swum two lengths of the pool doing the crawl stroke in under the allotted time; he retrieved a quarter from the bottom of the deep end, and was about to demonstrate a proper flip turn when Jake walked into the Davis's backyard. Mrs. Davis was beside him, looking distressed.

"What's up," he called from the deep end.
"Jamal, it's your grandmother."

CHAPTER TWELVE

"What, what about her? Is she ok?"

"No, Jamal, she's in the hospital. A neighbor called the ambulance. They think she had a stroke. Get dressed. We'll drive to Dallas and see what's going on."

They were on the road in 10 minutes. The kids all said "hope your grandmother is all right," and "Sorry, Jamal." Somehow in the short time it took Jamal to get dressed, Mrs. Davis managed to pack them sandwiches and fruit for the road, not that Jamal nor Jake felt like eating.

By the time, they got to the highway, Jake had told Jamal all he knew: The neighbor, Mrs. Gonzales and his grandmother were having coffee. G-mama had planned on watching her toddler son while Mrs. Gonzales ran to the store. G-mama dropped her coffee cup and when she tried to apologize, her words made no sense. Mrs. Gonzales called an ambulance. After the ambulance left, she went into G-mama's apartment and called Ms. Truwell.

"Apparently, your grandmother is pretty close with this neighbor and has told her all about you and the

Pathway Project so she knew about Mrs. Truwell. She found her number posted by the phone. My number was there too, but she called Mrs. Truwell first and Mrs. Truwell said she would call us.

"I was on my way to the hardware store when she called. I'm really glad, by the way, that you talked me into getting this smart phone. Mrs. Truwell says she's at St. Joesph's Hospital on Elm. Here," He handed Jamal his new phone, "can you get directions?"

It took them two hours to get to the hospital. Once inside they found a hospital volunteer who efficiently directed them to the right floor. She was in the ICU. They found Emma Truwell in the ICU waiting room.

"Oh, Jake, Jamal, I'm so glad you're here. I saw your grandmother for a couple minutes. She's quite weak. The doctor said it was a good thing she got here so quickly. They were able to administer a medicine called...here I wrote it down...iPA. It lowers blood pressure right away and can prevent some damage." Ms. Truwell gave him a quick hug. "I'm sure you can see her. Go through those doors. You have to ring in on the pad on the wall on the right side of the door."

They did as she directed. When they rang, someone on speaker asked who they were there to see. The doors were opened for them and a nurse met them as they walked in.

"Hello, I'm Leslie Simmons, one of the people taking care of Mrs. Jackson. Dr. Lui is her primary and with her now. You can go on in, Room 2218.

The ICU rooms formed a circle around the nurses' station. The rooms weren't like regular hospital rooms. The top half of each room was glass. Some had curtains pulled over the glass, but most didn't. They continued walking around the nurses' station quickly found Room 2218. A man and two women were in the room with her.

"J – J – J – J Grandson. It shlow – It's good see you." Jamal was shocked at her appearance. She'd shrunk. She looked tiny and fragile. The left side of her face drooped.

"I'm Dr. Lui," said one of the woman. She shook Jame's and then Jamal's hand. "Your grandmother suffered a stroke early this morning. Fortunately we were able to treat her right away, so we may have been able to minimize brain damage and other potential complications. We'll keep her in ICU for at least 24 hours. If she improves sufficiently, we'll then transfer her to our stroke ward on the third floor." Though not unfriendly, the woman was all business, not a great bedside manner.

"I need to go now, but I'll be back later this evening." Dr. Lui was pleasant, but seemed to be 'all business.'"

"I know she's happy to see you, but please keep your visit short. She needs to rest. If you have questions or concerns when I'm not here," she glanced at the white board on the wall, "her nurse, Leslie Simmons, will be able to help you."

Jamal had been looking at his G-mama the whole time, trying very hard not to cry.

"I now I rest but you stay. Love you. Fine soon." She patted his arm with her right hand as she struggled to talk.

It looked to Jake that that speech pretty much wore her out. "Jamal, we do need to let your grandmother have her rest. Why don't we..."

"I'd like to stay here a little longer if that's ok." Jamal looked at his grandmother who nodded. "I won't tire her out. I promise. I'll just sit here."

"You ---- talk ----tell me ------summer"

So Jake went out to talk with Ms. Truwell and Jamal told G-mama about roping and swimming lessons. She fell asleep and began to snore while he was was talking about Sadie liking carrots.

Leslie Simmons suggested that since she was sleeping Jamal could go out to waiting room for a while, maybe get a soda. He found Jake and Ms. Truwell in the waiting room.

"She's asleep"

"She needs to rest, Jamal. Let's take a walk outside. We'll be back before she wakes up."

Hand in his pockets, Jamal accompanied Jake and Ms. Truwell down the hall, down the elevator and out past the gift shop and out into a court yard. It was pretty warm, but they found a bench in the shade.

"She looks really, really sick." Jamal paused looked down at the ground and asked the question he was afraid to ask. "Is she gonna die?"

Ms. Truwell opened her mouth to answer, but Jake spoke first, "Jamal, from everything I heard, I think she is going to recover. No promises, but I really think no one is thinking 'this is it'. She is seriously ill, but I really think she'll get better.

He took a deep breathe and went on, "You know I've had some experience with hospitals. My dad died from a congenital heart problem. He went fast. But my mom, well, it's hard to talk about, but she was in the last time for two weeks. It was difficult. They made her as comfortable as possible. We knew she was dying. This, this feels different. Your grandmother is really sick, but nobody is acting like she's dying. You can tell, really."

Jamal believed him, partly because it sounded true, but mostly because he needed it to be true.

They went to the truck to get the sandwiches Mrs. Davis had packed them while Ms. Truwell picked up some sweet iced tea from the hospital cafeteria. They met back at the shady bench and had a picnic balancing the food on their knees.

"I'm not here in an official capacity," Ms. Truwell said after they'd eaten, but I like your gramma, Jamal. Over this summer we've become friends. The hospital will assign one of their social workers to her. After her hospital stay, she will need rehab for movement and speech. It probably seems overwhelming, but she really is getting good care.

The next couple of days Jake and Jamal stayed in Dallas. Jake wanted to get a hotel but Miss Jacquoline would not allow them to when she had a perfectly good apartment that was currently empty. After one night on the sofa Jake craved a hotel bed, but realized that Jamal needed to be in his own house around the familiar.

Mrs. Gonzales came over the first night. Jake thanked her for quickly calling the ambulance. "You know, since she was diagnosed so quickly, they were able to give her this medicine that can stop the damage a stroke can cause. If you had waited, they wouldn't have been able to give her this medicine.

"Oh, I am so glad. You know you never are sure what to do, but Mrs Jackson, you know, she just looked so, so bad. I was really scared for her."

After 24 hours, Miss Jacquoline, as all the staff had taken to call her, was moved to the stroke ward where she was monitored and started on OT (occupational therapy), and PT (physical therapy). A speech and language therapist came in to evaluate her needs. On the fourth day of her stay in the stroke ward, a strategy meeting was called. Her room was crowded with staff: Dr. Lui, PT, OT, speech and language, and the hospital social worker (with clipboard), and civilians: Jamal, Jake and G-mama.

"Miss Jacquoline, you are making very good progress. In fact we are planning on kicking you out! Of course, you are not ready to go home so I will set you up at Hacienda Manor and Rehabilitation facility." The hospital social worker seemed to be in charge of the meeting. "It's on Clarkson about three miles from here."

"How – how – how long?" G-mama asked. You could tell she was worried.

"It's very hard to give you a definitive answer to that. You understand, many patients need, oh, four to six weeks in the skilled nursing section. Medicare will cover most all of it. You continue with OT, PT, and speech and language while you are in the skilled care section though with different personnel than you have in the hospital. There is an assisted living section at Hacienda also. You would be transferred to assisted living when you 'graduate' from skilled nursing but still can't live independently.

G-mama still looked worried.

"I've looked over all your reports," the social worker now addressed the staff in the room. "I'm not missing anything, am I? We're all in agreement?" Heads nodded. "Thank you all for coming."

Dr. Lui, PT, OT and speech and language wandered out the door.

The hospital social worker now turned to Jamel, "Jamal, we have your grandmother pretty well set up, but now we need to deal with you and where you will be living"

"Can't I just stay in our apartment until my gramma comes home?"

"No, I'm sorry. You are a minor and can't live unsupervised."

"What about Mrs. Gonzales, our neighbor?"

"I'm afraid it's a bit more complicated than that. Your grandmother rents your place throught Affordable Housing Section 8. Since she will be vacating her apartment for more than a month without qualifying extenuating circumstances, she has to give it up. The state won't allow her to 'double dip' for housing. The Hacienda will be her new residence paid for by federal and state funds." She took a moment to let that sink in and then continued. There is a group home for teenagers within walking distance of Hacienda. That's where you would need to go."

"How about that emancipated minor thing. Could I do that and stay in my apartment?"

Though she wondered how Jamal knew about emancipation of minors, she didn't ask, instead she said, "Even if you emancipated, Jamal, you wouldn't qualifty for Section 8. You couldn't stay in the apartment.

Jamal was miserable. This was totally unanticipated. He felt like every time he recovered from a blow, a harder hit comes his way. He turned to his grandmother. She had tears in her eyes, "So sorry, Jamal, so sorry, can't, don't know another way."

"Your grandmother and I had a long talk before the meeting. As you know a long conversation is still hard for her, but we spent the entire morning hashing it out. This was truly the best solution. You will be needing a caseworker also, Jamal. It won't be me. I'm with the hospital. Since you've already worked with Emma Truwell and she works for the state, she has agreed to add you to her regular caseload, the one she has in addition to the Pathway Project.

"Mr. Litchfield, you are not family, but if you could help clear out the apartment it would be a godsend. If you can't, I'll contact the Dallas Volunteer Bureau and see what they can do. I checked with Section 8. We have three weeks to vacate.

Jamal felt he should be strong for G-mama, but how could he with his world falling apart.

"We'll give you some time alone to talk about this." The social worker looked pointedly at Jake and opened the hospital room door for him. As the door was closing behind them, Jake heard Mrs. Jackson assuring Jamal that Ms. Truwell had researched the group home and that it was a good place for him. He could hear her trying to convince him and herself. They were in a tough situation.

On his way downstairs, Jake called Ms. Truwell on his cell phone. They talked about the obvious: where Jamal would live after the Pathway Project ended. Jake knew that he could, perhaps should, offer to have Jamal stay with him. Could he become a permanent guardian for a teenager? Would it be the best thing for Jamal? He really needed to think about this. Whatever conclusion he came to, he would discuss it with Jamal tonight.

Maybe it was being in the hospital that made him think about his mom. She had been on his mind the last several days. He wished she were still around. She had left this earth way too early. He would have appreciated talking all of this over with her. He tried to imagine what advice she would have for him.

Jamal met up with him in the hospital cafeteria. Jake had found a paper and was on his second cup of coffee. Jamal plopped into a chair on the opposite side of the small table. He looked at Jake. Ok, no good reason to delay this conversation except that it was going to be difficult, uncomfortable and he really didn't want to see the disappointment in Jamal's eyes. The poor kid had gone through so much already. Was there any way of saying this that won't hurt him? Probably not.

"Jamal, I think you may find the group home a positive move." He sounded like a disinterested bureaucrat, not at all like someone who cared about this boy....try again Jake... "You might be thinking that you could stay in Clayton Springs on the ranch, but there are lots of reasons the group home is a better idea. First of all you will be close to your grandmother. You could visit her after school. The home is run by good people, Ms. Truwell told me about it. I think you will fit in well."

"So everyone knew about this before me," thought Jamal. "I guess the adults in charge have planned my life and I don't have a choice. That's it then"

"Let's take a look at this group home. We'll just drop in. That way we'll get a realistic feel for the place. I have the address. The group home 'parents' are Arlene and Dave Morgan."

They drove the three miles and found the place. It was a tidy two story. It even had a white picket fence. There were three youngsters out front, a boy around seven on a Big Wheel and two boys a little younger playing with dump trucks in a sand pit. Jake and Jamal rang the bell. A woman answered. It was Arlene. She was not at all put out by their dropping in though she asked if they could talk in the kitchen because she was in the middle of putting dinner together in a huge crockpot.

"I do this a couple times a week. Then at dinner time we add rolls and a salad and it's almost like some one else has made the meal."

The place was clean and well kept. Arlene seemed genuinely warm and welcoming. They didn't get to meet Dave. He was at soccer practice with several of the boys.

Now the group home was not an unknown. He still didn't want to go, but now he knew he could and would do it. Unfortunately, it would be out of his old school area, so he would be starting a new middle school in September. He hoped they had an advanced geometry class.

Jake needed to go back to the ranch. Mrs. Gonzales offered to watch Jamal. Jamal was pulled both ways. He wanted to stay in Dallas to be with his grandmother (he could take the 10B bus from his apartment building to the hospital) but he also wanted to go back to Clayton Springs to be at the ranch and see Sadie and his friends. Jake let Jamal decide. He opted to stay with Mrs. Gonzales. Jake was a little hurt and a little relieved.

After two days he was back in Dallas. Manual was doing a good job of keeping things up at the ranch so Jake felt ok about being away. He'd kept in touch with Jamal by phone. He'd been calling the land line at Mrs. Gonzales's place, but he wanted to be able to get a hold of Jamal directly, so he stopped at T-Mobile and added a second phone to his plan.

The next week when they weren't at the hospital, they were at the apartment packing up. Even though it was a tiny place, it took an amazing number of boxes to put away the Jackson's belongings. Jake rented an eight by ten storage unit. All of their furniture and kitchen ware would go in there. Jamal kept out his stuff (5 boxes) and they put aside clothes, pictures, and personal items (3 boxes) Jacquoline would take to Hacienda. Jake paid for the storage unit for a year.

If or when Jacquoline recovered sufficiently to live on her own, Jake promised he would come help them move to a new place. Everyone was hopeful that this would happen in less than six months. Jamal's grandmother was making excellent progress and making a herculean effort with OT, PT and Speech and language.

In the beginning of August Ms. Jacquoline moved to Hacienda Rehabilitation facility. She had her choice of going by ambulance or private vehicle. She asked Jake if he would drive her and he was pleased to oblige. It was a little hard getting her into the cab of the pick up.

"That's one big step Jake!" But with Jake helping on one side and Herman the six foot four, 250 pound nurse's assistant on the other, they whisked her right up there.

"Getting down is always easier, ma'am. You behave yourself at Hacienda...no dancing' 'til the second night." Herman had grown quite fond of Ms. Jacquoline during her stay. "We'll miss you, but don't you come back, you hear!"

Jake dreaded going to Hacienda. He's vision of a nursing home, especially one funded by the government was a dreary, smelly, barely tolerable place, but when he arrived, he was pleasantly surprised—boarding on shock. It was light, and, though a bit dated looking, clean and airy. There were flowers in the lobby. The grounds had pathways through a large lawn and several flower beds. Miss Jacquoline would be sharing a room with Miss Millie who had been there for two weeks and was eager to share all her knowledge of the place with her new roomie. She knew which of the staff were sweet on each other, what was the best dessert...the apple strudel was heaven but stay away from the cheesecake, Hon. And if Miss Jacquoline didn't know how to play bridge, well she and Nancy and Deb would be teaching her. Nancy and Deb had graduated to assisted living in the north building, but they came over every afternoon. "Thanks goodness you are here. I just know we are going to get along famously. I can tell I'm an excellent judge of people."

Miss Millie was recovering from a hip replacement. She had no problem with speech and language except perhaps an overabundance of it. She had already made arrangements to stay permanently in the assisted living section after she graduated.

"Three meals a day that I don't have to cook, a nice room they'll clean once a week and good people. Oh, Jackie, you are going to love it. Everyone's hesitant at first, but the place will win you over."

No one had ever called his G-mama "Jackie" but it seemed she had unwittingly joined a senior sorority and gotten a new name.

Jake brought in her three boxes and set things up around her room under her direction. They all ate lunch in the cafeteria-- white table clothes---fancy.

"You enjoy your last week at the ranch," G-mama's speech had improved tremendously. There was a slight slur, but she hardly had to "brain hunt" for words anymore. "F- f-f-finish those swim lessons. I want a report and give my love to your friend." She meant Devon, of course, but she rarely mentioned him and never by name.

CHAPTER THIRTEEN

Jamal's last week in Clayton Springs was bittersweet. He rode Sadie most every day. He successfully lassoed the fence point.

At the Davis's house after his final swim lesson, they had dinner. Mrs. Davis served artichokes and Jamal gave Devon step by step instructions on how to eat them and to especially avoid the fuzzy part. Mr. Davis enrolled Devon at Clayton Springs. (His paperwork said Darwin Brooks, but his teachers would be told that he went by "Devon." He would be starting in a new special day class because he was so far behind in his reading and math skills. The teacher was young, but had a stellar reputation.

"I guess she's single and pretty too, Devon told Jamal, Not that I care, but I'm thinking me and Brenda could work on getting her set-up with Jake."

The morning he left, he went to the barn and gave Sadie carrots and told her how much he would miss her, but that Jake had promised he could come back next summer and maybe a weekend or two in the fall. He would be keeping the cell phone so he could call G-mama and Jake any time he wanted.

"You could call Vicki too," said Jake. "I think she might be a little sweet on you." At first that statement shocked Jamal and then he decided that Jake was out to lunch with that idea.

They made it to Dallas midday and stopped by Hacienda for a short visit. They found "Jackie," Millie, Nancy and Paula in the rec room discussing the proper response to a one no trump opening bid. G-mama was looking better. She had gained a bit of weight, but she needed a wheelchair to get around most of the time. Her left leg was being uncooperative, but she was working hard on it in PT.

"You off to the Morgans now? You behave yourself, best manners. Promise?"

"Yes, G-mama," Jamal could and would do it. He was determined to make it work. He kept giving himself mental pep-talks so that he wouldn't sink into melancholy.

They drove up to the group home. Both Arlene and Dave were there to greet him. Jake brought his five boxes in from the truck and set them in a corner of Jamal's shared room. He'd deal with them later.

And then it was time to go.

"I'll miss you, Jamal. I wish, you know, but..."

"Yeah, I know."

They started to shake hands, but before either of them realized it, they were in a bear hug.

"Call tonight, ok? I want to hear about your first day." and then he was back in the truck headed down the road.

"Unpack later, Jamal," Arlene said as they watch Jake's truck take a left at the corner. Richard and Terry are playing horse out back. They'd like a third.

Her "horse" comment had him flash a vision of Sadie on the Morgan's back lawn. Then he quickly realized she was talking about shooting hoops.

"Sure," and he headed back to join his new roommates. They were a bit shy with each other at first, but you don't have to have a conversation while playing basketball.

David watched from the kitchen window while he worked on the salad. "Looks like they're getting along ok. 'course anybody can get along with Richard. Maybe he'll get Terry to start talking."

"Your lips to God's ear," Arlene replied.

They finished their game of horse and played two more.

"Wash your hands for dinner," Arlene called as they came in the back door. "Family meeting after dinner." Jamal was edgy. He felt like a guest who wasn't a guest which was, of course, how every new boy felt the first day. They either acted out for the first week or silently watched everything until they were comfortable. Arlene and Dave had the "becoming familiar" period down pat. Jamal was going to be a quiet one. They would do introductions and house rules at the family meeting after dinner. Jamal's name would be added to the chore chart and he would be shown where everything was. The rest was up to him.

He got along with Richard and Terry. Richard was friendly but Jamal didn't connect with him like he did with Brenda and Vicki. He quickly learned that if he was missing anything he should look for it in Terry's drawers.

"Sticky hands. He means no harm. Can't help himself." was how it was explained to Jamal. Terry would just watch and look a little sad when one of the boys fished through his drawers and came up with their missing item.

Jamal followed the rules: lights out at 10 (it would go to 9 when school started); clean up the play room after dinner; complete your chores (cleaning the bathroom was the worst, but it worked out that you only had to do it once a week); keep your part of your bedroom tidy; no phone or texting during dinner; be polite and kind to one another; help take care of the younger kids.

School started the Wednesday after Labor Day. Dave planned to take Jamal in the first day.

Part of his obligation to the Pathway Project was to give a short presentation to the East Dallas Thursday Rotary Club. They had sponsored four teenagers in the program. Jamal worked on a speech telling about his summer experience and thanking them for the opportunity. It was going to be sort of a big deal. It was a lunch meeting and the four teenagers were going to present after the abbreviated Rotary meeting during lunch. The teenagers families and host families were invited. Jamal's table for 10 was going to be full. The Davises were coming, and, of course, Jake. Ms. Truwell was coming as a Pathway representative and as a friend. She would pick up G-mama and then swing by to pick up Jamal. Mayor Jenkins called Jake on the Tuesday before and told him that she would be coming and that he would be driving her. That didn't surprise him much. MaryEllen always wanted to be part of the action.

Ms. Truwell came by at 10 to pick up Jamal. "No reason to be late, every reason to be early." They then went to Hacienda Rehab for G-mama. She was waiting in her room with her three friends.

"Hi, Jamal, this is a big day for you."

"We are so proud.'

"How do you like your grandmother's new hairdo?" They had been "fixing up" Jackie all morning. Millie was in charge of make-up. Deb and Nancy did her hair. Jamal could tell she was pretty happy with the way she looked. What was that? Green shiny stuff on her eyelids. Is that what old ladies wore? To him she sort of looked like his G-mama but fancy or, well, just different. He didn't think he would understand the whole make-up thing but he did understand that she enjoyed her friends fussing over her.

"You look pretty, G-mama."

"Why, thank you, Jamal." She patted her teased and sprayed hairdo and smiled at her friends. Deb used to run a beauty parlor. She is quite an expert."

"We want to hear your speech. Jackie says you will be talking in front of a whole room full of people. What are you going to say? Stand right there and pretend you are at the Rotary. Let's hear it."

Jamal looked at Ms. Truwell and his G-mama. "Good thing we started early. We have plenty of time and it will be good practice," was what Ms. Truwell said. G-mama didn't say anything, but gave him a lopsided smile letting him know that she would like to show him off to her friends.

He pulled his note cards from his back pocket, stood up straight and gave his speech.

"That was wonderful."

"Outstanding"

"Terrific. I'd vote for you if you ran for Congress." Sometimes Millie made no sense, but she loved to talk and was always nice.

"Ok, Miss Jacquoline lets be on our way." Jamal helped his grandmother into the wheelchair. They rolled her down the hall and out to the parking lot. Transfer from chair to car went smoothly. Jamal stowed the wheel chair into the trunk, thought about Devon's ride in that same trunk almost two months ago, and climbed into the back seat.

"Are you nervous, Jamal?"

"A little."

"Well, you did a marvelous job in front of your grandmother's friends. I like what you have to say. You'll be just fine."

They arrived at the restaurant a half hour before Rotary started. Ms. Truwell parked in a handicap spot using a temporary handicap placard she picked up at Hacienda. Jamal helped G-mama from the front seat and they went inside to find the meeting room. There were about a hundred people in the room and it was only half full. They looked around for their table and saw that the Davises, Jake and Mayor Jenkins were already at a large round table near the front. Jamal was surprised to see that Devon had come along with the Davis clan.

"Dude, should you be here in Dallas?"

"J-dawg, look at me. No one would recognize me." That was probably true. Devon's face had healed, but what made him look totally different was his cowboy hat, plaid shirt, jeans and boots. "Do I look like I'm from the city? Besides, I don't know many gang members that hang out at a rotary meeting." Even so, he was whispering and keeping his head down not looking at any one directly.

Jake stood up as Jamal came to the table. He waited for Jamal and Devon to finish and then gave him a hug. "Missed you kid."

"Yeah, me too."

"Miss Jacquoline, you are looking lovely!" G-mama nodded and gave Jake her post-stroke lopsided smile.

Everyone sat at the table and chatted until it was time for the presentations. Jamal was first. He walked to the podium at the front of the room, adjusted the microphone and pulled out his note cards.

"I know you have three other speeches to listen to and everyone wants to eat their lunches so I'll try to keep it brief." At this he paused, the audience chuckled and nodded. "Ladies and gentlemen of Rotary, I want to thank you for giving me the opportunity through the Pathway Project to experience a wonderful summer in Clayton Spring. I learned so much and met so many great people." Jamal went on to tell about leaning to ride, being in the choir at Clayton Springs Baptist Church and ended with a funny story about mounting Sadie backward and riding around the corral for twenty minutes until he could figure out how to get down.

He received a huge round of applause. Everyone at Jamal's table agreed that his speech was far superior to the other three.

Salad was served during the fourth presentation. Speech over, Jamal could finally relax and enjoy being with his Clayton Springs friends and family. He talked a little about the group home. During the dessert (ice cream sundaes), Jake looked at Ms. Truwell and then at Miss Jacquoline. They nodded at him and he said, "Jamal, would you please come with me for a couple minutes?"

"Sure." He left his melty sundae and went out the front door of the restaurant. There was a bench out front for people waiting for tables, reminiscent of the bench in the courtyard of the hospital.

"Jamal, I haven't been totally honest with you. It was a lie of omissiion." Jake paused. Jamal was very confused. "I talked with your grandmother and Ms. Truwell back when it became apparent that your gramma would be in rehab for quite a while.

"I wanted to offer to have you live with me right then, but your gramma and Ms. Truwell convinced me that you needed a choice. If you hadn't gone to the group home, it never would have been a real choice for you. Now that you've been there a while, you know what it is like. You know your roommates and house parents. You know the neighborhood and how close it is to go visit Miss Jacquoline at Hacienda.

"You also have a good idea of what living on the ranch with me would be like. Now you have a decision to make, an informed decision.

"One more thing, Jamal, I really want you to come live with me. I'm not just doing this for you. I'm doing it for me too, but it is your choice. Do what you think is best for you, not for me or for anyone else.

"The Morgans know about this. That's why they haven't registered you for school yet. But you have to decide now, today. Can you do that?"

"Wow, yeah. Let me think a minute."

"You got it." Jake got up and returned to the table. Jamal stayed at the bench.

"He's thinking about it."

"Good for him, not making a snap judgment."

Jamal walked back to the table ten minutes later. He had decided and felt good about his choice. He knew it was right for him.

He told the group at the table. Everyone smiled.

Mayor Jenkins, never a loss for words, looked at the adults at the table and said, "It's like in that Keith Richard song, 'sometimes if you try, you get what you need.'"

The adults nodded.

But Devon whispered to Jamal, "Keith Richards?"

Jamal whispered back with a grin, "I dunno. Maybe he's a country singer."